U0088079

@ 雅典文化

生活單字
萬用手冊

GLISH INCREASE YOU

OCABULARY

AN MAKE YOU FEEL GREAT ABOUT SPEAKING ENGLISH.

國家圖書館出版品預行編目資料

生活單字萬用手冊 / 張瑜凌編著
-- 二版 -- 新北市：雅典文化，民109.12
面； 公分 -- (行動學習；17)
ISBN 978-986-99431-1-6(平裝附光碟片)
1. 英語 2. 詞彙
805.12   109015868

行動學習系列 17

生活單字萬用手冊

編著／張瑜凌
責任編輯／張文娟
內文排版／鄭孝儀
封面設計／林鈺恆

法律顧問：方圓法律事務所／涂成樞律師

總經銷：永續圖書有限公司
永續圖書線上購物網
www.foreverbooks.com.tw

CVS代理／美璟文化有限公司
TEL：(02) 2723-9968
FAX：(02) 2723-9668

出版日／2020年12月

雅典文化

出版社
22103　新北市汐止區大同路三段194號9樓之1
TEL　(02) 8647-3663
FAX　(02) 8647-3660

【關於本書】

只會簡單的單字，也可以開口說英語！

你還在為無法開口說英語而煩惱嗎？每次遇到要開口說英語時，就會緊張、詞窮嗎？其實學英語真的不難，只要您能把握一個基本的原則：「提升單字的實力」。

「單字」就如同是語言架構的基礎工程，在英語學習階段中，增加腦袋中單字庫的容量，是穩紮穩打培養實力的首要步驟。

「生活單字萬用手冊」提供了 127 個單元的單字，並依照生活口語中使用的頻繁率，增加「生活實用例句」單元，讓您能夠依據單字表，應用在

英語生活口語之中。

除了「生活實用例句」之外，本書還增加「相關單字」單元，讓您能在同一時間瞭解相關性質的單字，目的也是為了增加您的單字實力。

此外，「生活單字萬用手冊」還有另一項法寶：「慣用語句」，主要是以英語的通俗用法、非正式用法或俚語為主題，教您一些平常書上看不到的英語應用，實用、簡單，又能充分表達語言的詞義。

秉持一貫的「真人發音、一對一學習」的精神，「生活單字萬用手冊」提供了全英語發音的 MP3，讓您能夠反覆閱聽、跟著老師的步調練習發音。

別以為要能出國才能說得一口流利的英語，只要循序漸進提升單字實力，充分掌握「單字＋例句」的學習方式，英語口語能力絕對 UP UP！

食物・餐點

料理

服裝

生活單字 萬用手冊

家庭生活

公共設施

交通

生活單字 萬用手冊

生活單字 萬用手冊

自然現象

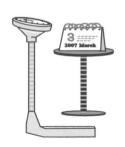

Unit 001 稱謂

我	I
我們	we
你、你們	you
他	he
她	she
它、牠	it
他們	they
我(受詞)	me
我們(受詞)	us
他(受詞)	him
她(受詞)	her
他們、它們(受詞)	them
我的(東西)	mine
我自己	myself
你(們)自己	yourself
他自己	himself
她自己	herself
他們自己	themselves

1

生活實用例句

1 I'm on my way home.
我正在回家了路上。

2 Would you like to have dinner with us?
你想和我們一起用餐嗎？

3 I will treat you.
我請客。

4 He is moving next week.
他下星期搬家。

5 Give me a hand, please.
請幫我一個忙。

6 Please ask her to call me back.
請她回我電話！

7 Will you wrap them up?
能請你幫我包裝它們嗎？

8 Tina and I both have red hair.
蒂娜和我都是紅頭髮。

2 相關單字

你(們)的(東西)	yours
他的(東西)	his
她的(東西)	hers
他們的(東西)	theirs
它的（東西）	its

3 慣用語句

▶ jerk

古怪的人

說明 表示某人是個糟糕、無用的人。

例 Tony is such a jerk -- he stole my lunch money!

湯尼是個混蛋，他偷了我午餐的錢。

Unit 002 長輩親屬

曾祖父	great-grand father
曾祖母	great-grand mother
祖父母	grandparents

祖父	grandfather
祖母	grandmother
叔公、舅公	granduncle
姑婆、姨婆	grandaunt
父母	parents
單親(父或母)	single parent
父	father
母	mother
公公、岳父	father-in-law
婆婆、岳母	mother-in-law
伯父、叔父、舅父	uncle
伯母、叔母、舅母	aunt
繼父	step-father
繼母	step-mother
養父母	adoptive parent
養父	adoptive father
養母	adoptive mother

1

生活實用例句

1 What's your mother's maide name?
你母親的娘家姓氏是什麼？

2 They are my grandparents.
他們是我的祖父母。

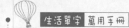
3 His parents live in New York.
他的父母親住在紐約。

4 Uncle David, where are you going?
大衛叔叔，你要去哪裡？

5 Her adoptive parents were farmers.
他的養父母是農夫。

6 They adopted David last September.
他們去年九月領養大衛。

2 相關單字

領養、收養	adopt
亡父	late father
亡母	late mother

Unit 003 同輩

夫妻、情侶	couple
配偶	spouse
丈夫	husband
妻子	wife
前夫	ex-husband
前妻	ex-wife
姊夫、妹夫、丈夫或	brother-in-law

妻子之兄弟	
嫂嫂、姑姑、丈夫或妻子的姊妹	sister-in-law
兄弟	brother
姐妹	sister
雙胞胎兄弟	twin brother
雙胞胎姊妹	twin sister
手足	sibling
堂(表)兄妹	cousin
異父(母)姊妹	step-sister
異父(母)兄弟	step-brother

生活實用例句

1. An elderly couple lives next door.
   有一對老夫婦住在隔壁。

2. I've never met Tina's husband.
   我從沒見過蒂娜的丈夫。

3. Her ex-husband kept their cat.
   她前夫擁有他們的貓。

4. Although never married, they lived together as husband and wife for fifty years.
   雖然沒有結婚，他們住在一起就像夫妻一樣長達五十年。

5 I have four siblings: three brothers and a sister.

我有四位兄弟姊妹：三個兄弟、一個姊妹。

6 My brother's wife and I both had babies around the same time.

我大嫂和我同時生小孩。

2 慣用語句

▶ rookie
新手

說明 在某個領域中是個新手，類似中文的「菜鳥」。

例 The older players taught the rookie how to play the game.

老球員教菜鳥如何打這場比賽。

Unit 004 晚輩親屬

小孩	kid
孩子	child (複數 children)
兒子	son

女兒	daughter
寶貝	baby
男孩	boy
女孩	girl
女婿	son-in-law
媳婦	daughter-in-law
雙胞胎	twin
外甥、姪兒	nephew
外甥女、姪女	niece
孫子女	grandchild
孫子	grandson
孫女	granddaughter
繼子	step-son
繼女	step-daughter
養子	adoptive son
養女	adoptive daughter

生活實用例句

1. How many kids do you have?
   你有幾個孩子？

2. I have an eight-year-old boy.
   我有一個八歲的兒子。

3. Tina and Phil have a daughter and three sons.
   蒂娜和菲爾有 個女兒、三個兒子。

4　Tom is a six-week-old baby.
　　湯姆是一個六個星期大的嬰兒。

5　They have a baby boy.
　　他們有一個小男嬰。

6　My sister has two sons.
　　我姊妹有一對雙胞胎。

7　Liz is my twin sister.
　　麗茲是我的雙胞胎姊妹。

8　I have two nephews and three
　　nieces.
　　我有兩個姪子、三個姪女。

9　In her will she left all her money to
　　her granddaughter.
　　她在遺囑中將所有的錢都留給了她的孫
　　女。

2 慣用語句

▶ in the slammer
坐牢

說明　slam 是指「砰一聲關上」，而 in
　　　the slmmer 是口語化「關在監獄」
　　　的意思。

例　Tony spent a few years in the
　　slammer for robbing a grocery store.
　　湯尼因為搶劫雜貨店而坐牢好幾年。

Unit 005 家族

家庭、家人	family
親戚、姻親	relatives
親戚	in-laws
血族、親戚	kinsfolk
出身、血統	origin
祖先(總稱)	ancestor
祖宗、祖先	ancestry
祖先	forebears
祖先(不一定有血緣)	forefather
家世	extraction
世代	generation
後代、後裔	descendant
子女、子孫、後代	offspring
子孫、後裔、子女	progeny
繼承人	heir
婚姻	marriage
家譜	family tree
單親家庭	single family
血緣	blood

1 生 活 實 用 例 句

1 How is your family?

你的家人好嗎？

2 They are my in-laws.

他們是我的親戚們。

3 All her relatives came to the wedding.

所有她的親戚都來參加婚禮。

4 He returned to Japan, where his mother's ancestors lived.

他回去他母親的故鄉日本。

5 There were three generations at the wedding - grandparents, parents, and children.

婚禮總共有三代出席，祖父母、父母、和孩子們！

6 My cousin Robert is the only heir to my uncle's fortune.

我表哥羅伯是我叔叔財產的唯一繼承人。

2 相關單字

這一代	the present generation
上一代	the past generation
下一代	the coming generation
代溝	generation gap

3 慣用語句

▶ on the same wavelength
相同頻道

說明 表示彼此有默契或是想法、觀念一致！

例 Peter and Tina have really been on the same wavelength lately -- they agree about almost everything.

最近彼得和蒂娜兩人很有默契，幾乎每件事他們的意見都是一致的。

Unit 006 男女之間

男朋友	boyfriend
女朋友	girlfriend
戀人	lover
新郎	groom
新娘	bride
戀情	relationship
相親	blind date
約會	date
結婚	marry
訂婚	engage
離婚	divorce
分居	separate
懷孕	pregnant
避孕	contraception
生理期	menstrual period
(女性生理期)痙攣	cramp
保險套	condom
墮胎	abortion

1

生活實用例句

1. Are you seeing someone?
   你有交往的對象嗎？

2. Are we lovers, or just friends?
   我們是戀人還是朋友？

3. Are we taking this relationship seriously, or just for fun?
   我們有要穩定交往，還是只是玩一玩的男女關係？

4. Marry me.
   嫁給我吧！

5. They just got married last month.
   他們上個月才剛結婚。

6. Anthony is engaged to Ann.
   安東尼和安訂婚了。

7. I missed my period.
   我的月經沒有來。

8. My period is irregular.
   我的經期不正常

9. I'm having a cramp.
   我經痛。

10. She decided to have an abortion.
    她決定要墮胎。

2 相關單字

生產	give birth
與某人交往	see someone
結婚的	get married
發生性關係	have sex
墮胎	have an abortion
分手	break up
一夜情	one night stand
一見鍾情	fall in love at first sight

3 慣用語句

▶ hottie

性感、吸引人的女性

說明 多半形容女子性感、漂亮，類似中文「辣妹」、「正妹」的敘述。

例 My girlfriend is a real hottie.
我的女友真是個辣妹。

男性	male
男性	man(複數 men)
女性	female
女性	woman (複數 women)
單身者/單身的	single
寡婦	widow
鰥夫	widower
朋友	friend
初學走路的小孩	toddler
嬰幼兒(會行走之前的)	infant
先生(冠於姓氏前)	Mr.
太太(冠於姓氏前)	Mrs.
小姐(冠於姓氏前)	Miss
先生(用於稱呼)	sir
夫人(用於稱呼)	madam
紳士(用於稱呼)	gentleman
淑女(用於稱呼)	lady
(招待客人的)主人	host
(招待客人的)女主人	hostess
客人	guest

1

生活實用例句

1. He's been single for so long, I don't think he'll ever marry.

   他都單身這麼久了，我不認為他會結婚。

2. His widowed mother brought him up.

   他的寡母把他撫養成人。

3. My widowed uncle lives upstairs.

   我喪偶的叔叔住在樓上。

4. I will pick my girlfriend up tomorrow.

   我明天會去接我的女朋友。

5. Are these toys suitable for toddlers?

   這些玩具適合嬰孩嗎？

6. Good afternoon, Mr. Baker.

   午安，貝克先生。

7. May I help you, madam?

   女士，需要我幫忙嗎？

8. Ladies and gentlemen, may I have your attention, please.

   各位先生、各位女士，請注意！

2 相關單字

雅痞	yuppie
監護人	tutor
監護人	guardian
囚犯	prisoner
罪犯	criminal
叛亂者	rebel
消費者、用戶	consumer
十七、八歲的男孩	boy in his late teens
早起的人	early riser
清早的拜訪者	early visitor

3 慣用語句

▶ **sugar daddy**

親密愛人

說明 這裡可不是指「父親」的角色，而是指為維持一段戀愛關係而付出金錢或禮物的男性。

例 My sugar daddy bought me a new car!

我的親密愛人買給我一部新車。

Unit 008 職業(一)

職業	occupation
工作	job
(全體)工作人員	staff
傭人、服務生	servant
清潔工	house cleaner
清潔女工	cleaning maid
潛水員	aquanaut
飛行員、領航員	pilot
太空人	astronaut
經紀人	agent
運動員	athlete
警衛	security guard
偵探	detective
法官	judge
律師	attorney
律師	lawyer
廚子	cook
廚師	chef
幫手(餐廳做端菜、收碗盤的人)	bus boy/bus girl

1

生活實用例句

1 She joined the staff of the Smithsonian Institution in 2002.

她在 2002 年加入 Smithsonian 機構成為他們的一員。

2 Mr. Baker is a civil servant.

貝克先生任職於國家機構。

3 He's a sports agent and has a lot of basketball players as clients.

他是一位運動經紀人，他有許多棒球球員的委託人。

4 The firm has 1000 employees.

這家公司有一千名員工。

5 Mr. Baker is his defense attorney.

貝克先生是他的辯護律師。

6 I want to see my lawyer before I say anything.

在我發言前，我想要見我的律師。

7 John is an airline pilot.

約翰是一位飛機駕駛。

8 He's an excellent cook.

他是一位很棒的廚師。

相關單字

代表	representative
委託人	client
受僱者	employee
發言人	spokesman

慣用語句

▶ icky

黏膩的

說明 表示「黏膩」、「甜得發膩」的意思。

例 Your kitchen is so icky! Why don't you clean it up?

你的廚房油膩膩的！你怎麼不清洗一下呢？

職業(二)

男侍者	waiter
女服務生	waitress
女裁縫	seamstress
熨燙衣服者	ironer
歌手	singer
舞蹈家	dancer
畫家、油漆工	painter
教師	teacher
作家	writer
記者	reporter
廣播員	announcer
工人	worker
農夫	farmer
工程師	engineer
哲學家	philosopher
探險家	explorer
律師	lawyer
駕駛員	driver
麵包師	baker
屠夫	butcher
軍人	soldier

生活單字 萬用手冊

警員	police officer
消防人員	fire fighter
臨時的保姆	baby-sitter
攝影師	photographer
作曲家	composer
(搬運行李的)侍應生	porter
鉛管工、水電工	plumber

1 生活實用例句

1. The engineer is coming to repair our phone tomorrow morning.
   明天早上工程師要來修理我們的電話。

2. Anthony is an Arctic explorer.
   安東尼是北極探險家。

3. Our baby-sitter is from the local college.
   我們的褓母是來自當地大學。

4. The waiter came to take their order.
   男侍來服侍他們點菜。

5. His mother is an opera singer.
   他的母親是一位歌劇演唱家。

6. My husband is a history teacher at the local school.
   我丈夫是本地學校的一位歷史教師。

7 He is a rice farmer.
他是一位稻農。

8 He is a taxi driver.
他是一位計程車司機。

2 相關單字

員工	worker
作者	writer
搶劫者、強盜	robber
劫機犯	hijacker
研究員	researcher
修理者	repairer
店主	shopkeeper
書商	bookseller
製造商	manufacturer
設計者	designer
顧客、客戶	customer
僱主	employer
賣方	seller
買方	buyer
簿記員	bookkeeper
計時員	timekeeper
贏家	winner
輸家	loser
保鏢	bouncer
使用炸彈的人、轟炸機	bomber

3 慣用語句

▶ baby-sit
臨時看顧幼童

說明 就像「坐在小嬰兒旁邊」的字面意思，表示臨時受顧於照顧小嬰兒或幼童。

衍生 baby-sitter 臨時保姆

例 I'm going to baby-sit on Tuesday night.

星期二晚上我要去當褓母。

Unit 010 職業(三)

教授	professor
導演	director
編者	editor
作者、作家	author
醫生、博士	doctor
裁縫師	tailor
小販、賣主	vendor
接線生、操作者	operator

雕刻家	sculptor
管理者、指導者	supervisor
水手	sailor
陸海軍人	soldiers and sailors
男演員	actor
女演員	actress

1

生活實用例句

1. Mr. Baker is a history professor.
   貝克先生是一位歷史學教授。

2. A director is also a person who tells actors in a movie or play how to play their parts.
   導演就是一部電影演或戲劇中，告訴演員如何詮釋他們的角色的人。

3. Mark Twain is my favorite author.
   馬克·吐溫是我最喜愛的作家。

4. What did the doctor say?
   醫生說了什麼？

5. Our company deals with many vendors of women's clothing.
   我們公司和許多女裝攤販溝通協調。

6 I am a machine operator.
我是一位機器操作員。

7 The play has a cast of six actors.
這部戲有六位演員的卡司。

8 My dad is a sailor.
我父親是一位船員。

2 相關單字

拜訪者	visitor
主管	superior
資深者	senior
資淺者	junior
視察員、檢查員	inspector
競爭者、對手	competitor

3 慣用語句

▶ in a funk
沮喪

說明 口語化用法，funk 是「畏縮」、「恐懼」的意思。

類似 feel blue　心情憂鬱

例 Tina is in a funk about her new haircut. She thinks it's much too short.
蒂娜對於新髮型很沮喪。她認為太短了！

Unit 011　職業(四)

漁夫	fisherman
郵差	mailman
警察	policeman
工匠	craftsman
軍人	serviceman
船員、水手	seaman
工匠、技工	artisan
圖書管理員	librarian
音樂家	musician
魔術師	magician
政治家	politician
數學家	mathematician
統計學家	statistician
內科醫師	physician
藥劑師	pharmacist
雜誌記者	journalist
鋼琴家	pianist
接待員	receptionist
分析家	specialist
語言學家	linguist
植物學家	botanist

經濟學家	economist
化學家	chemist
科學家	scientist
物理學家	physicist
生物學家	biologist
生理學家	physiologist
考古學家	archaeologist
地質學家	geologist
動物學家	zoologist
藝術家、美術家	artist
打字員	typist
分析師	analyst

1 生活實用例句

1. Maine fishermen are finding it difficult to make a living.
   緬因州的漁民生活困苦。

2. The mailman delivers letters and parcels every morning.
   郵差每天早晨遞送信件和包裹。

3. My brother is a jazz musician.
   我的兄弟是一位爵士音樂家。

4. I want to be a magician.
   我想要成為魔術師。

5　Are you a pianist?
　　你是鋼琴家嗎？

② 慣用語句

▶ croak
死亡

說明　croak是俚語「死亡」的意思，croak
有另一意是「青蛙呱呱叫」，兩種
意思之間的關連，是不是和中文「翹
辮」（口語「死亡」）很像呢？

例　After grandpa croaked, I inherited his
house.
祖父去世後，我繼承了他的房子。

Unit 012　職業（五）

老闆	boss
商人	merchant
劇作家	playwright
建築師	architect
模特兒	model
詩人	poet
男性空服員	steward

空中小姐	stewardess
外科醫生	surgeon
護士	nurse
導遊	guide
辦事員、職員	clerk

1 生活實用例句

1 A guide will show you round the Palace.

導遊將會陪你們參觀宮殿。

2 I'll ask my boss if I can take the afternoon off.

我會請示我的老闆,確認我下午是否可以請假。

3 Is Mr. Baker a brain surgeon or heart surgeon?

貝克先生是腦科醫師或是心臟科醫師?

4 Our tour guide in Rome was a lovely young woman who spoke perfect English.

我們在羅馬的導遊是一位年輕漂亮的女性,她會説很棒的英文。

5 He's one of the greatest poets.

他是偉大的詩人之一。

6 The sales clerk helped me find a sweater in my size.

銷售員有幫忙找出適合我的尺寸的毛衣。

2 相關單字

典範	role model
銷售人員	sales clerk
同事	colleague
同事、伙伴	fellow

3 慣用語句

▶ kick your ass

討打

說明 俚語用法，字面意思就是「踢你的屁股」的意思。

類似 your ass　　你自己

例 Don't mess with the bouncer unless you want him to kick your ass.

不要去逗弄保鑣，除非你想討打！

例 Get your ass in my office now!

你現在就來我的辦公室！

Unit 013 行政管理職務

董事長	president
總經理	general manager
經理	manager
管理者	administrator
主管	supervisor
助理	assistant
秘書	secretary
企畫人員	project staff
人事經理	personnel manager
人力資源部經理	human resources manager
培訓專家	trainer
生產經理	production manager
公共關係經理	public relations manager
顧問	consultant
高級顧問	senior consultant
品質控制員	QC inspector

1 生活實用例句

1 The company's board of directors will name a new president at its next meeting.

公司的董事會將指派下一次會議的董事。

2 I have to get off the phone – my supervisor just walked into the office.

我要掛電話了，我的主管剛剛走進辦公室了。

3 Mrs. Baker is his secretary.

貝克女士是他的秘書。

4 He is the manager of a supermarket.

他是行銷部門主管。

2 相關單字

總統	president
副總統	vice president

3 慣用語句

▶ eat lead

開槍

說明 子彈是由 lead（鉛）所製造的，eat lead 意指「對某人開槍射擊」的意思，中文的口語化說法就是「吃顆子彈」。

例 "Eat lead!" yelled the bank robber as he fired his gun at the police outside.

「吃我一顆子彈吧！」銀行搶匪對著外面的警察開槍喊道！

Unit 014　工程技術職務

程式設計師	programmer
電腦操作員	computer operator
系統分析員	systems analyst
系統操作員	systems operator
技術員	technician
工程師	engineer
總工程師	chief engineer
電腦工程師	computer engineer

顧問工程師	consulting engineer
軟體工程師	software engineer

1

生活實用例句

1. He is an engineer at a large electronics company.
   他是一家大型電器公司的工程師。
2. Adams is an X-ray technician.
   亞當斯是一位 X 光的技術人員。
3. My husband is a laboratory technician.
   我丈夫是一位實驗室的技術人員。

2 慣用語句

▶ ax

解職

說明	ax 除了是「斧頭」、「電吉他」之外，還有「解職」的意思。
應用	get the ax	解雇
類似	get fired	炒魷魚

例 Three staff members got the ax yesterday.

有三位員工昨天遭到解雇。

Unit 015 商業會計職務

會計員、會計師	accountant
查賬員	auditor
簿記員	bookkeeper
出口人員	export clerk
外銷員	export sales staff
財務分析員	financial analyst
市場分析員	market analyst
市場研究員	market researcher
銷售代表	marketing representative
採購員	purchaser
業務經理	business manager
外銷部經理	export sales manager
業務助理	business assistant

1
生 活 實 用 例 句

1. I am a tax accountant.
   我是一位稅法會計師。
2. A good bookkeeper does careful work.
   好的簿記員必須工作仔細！
3. Software purchasers have reported problems with the product.
   軟體採購員已經呈報產品的問題了。

2
慣 用 語 句

▶ be on cloud nine
興奮、高興

說明 來源自雲為天堂的一部份，你踏在越高的雲端上，表示越接近越興奮、高興的狀態。

例 I was on cloud nine after I got the promotion.
我很高興我升遷了。

Unit 016 文化教育職務

大學校長	president
美國私立學校校長	headmaster
美國私立學校女校長	headmistress
教授	professor
導師	supervisor
講師	lecturer
研究員	researcher
總編輯	chief editor
編輯	editor
報刊專欄作家	columnist
口譯員	interpreter
筆譯員、翻譯者	translator
記者	reporter

1 相關單字

1 Professor Stephen Hawking is coming back.
史蒂芬華金教授正要回來。

2 He is a sociology professor.
他是一位社會學教授。

3 She's a senior editor of a publishing company.

她是一位出版公司的資深編輯。

4 Who is the editor of the Times?

誰是目前 Time 雜誌的編輯？

5 She's a columnist for USA Today.

她是 USA Today 的專欄作家。

6 David is a sports columnist.

大衛是運動專欄作家。

7 Susan is a gossip columnist.

蘇珊是八卦版專欄作家。

8 He's a noted interpreter of traditional Irish music.

他是有名的傳統愛爾蘭音樂的口譯員。

9 He is a translator at the UN.

他在聯合國擔任翻譯職務。

2 慣用語句

▶ jumpy

提心吊膽的

說明 jump 是「彈跳」的意思，而 jumpy 是指因為恐懼或害怕而不安的意思。

例 I'm always a little bit jumpy when I walk by the graveyard at night.

當我晚上經過墓園時，我總是提心吊膽的。

Unit 017 飲食

吃(食物)	eat
吃(食物、飲料)	have
喝(飲料)	drink
吸食	suck
啜飲(用吸管)	sip
咬、一口	bite
嚼碎	chew
吞嚥	swallow
聞	smell
品嚐、味道	taste
吃(藥)、品嚐	take
飲食	diet
一餐	meal
早餐	breakfast
早午餐	brunch
午餐	lunch
晚餐、正餐	dinner
晚餐	supper
一盤(菜)	dish (複數dishes)
一份食物	help

一客、一杯(食物)	serving
一份(食物)	portion

1 生活實用例句

1. What are we going to have?
   我們要吃什麼？

2. Would you like to have dinner with us?
   你想和我們一起用餐嗎？

3. How about going out for dinner?
   出去吃晚餐如何？

4. Can I have a bite?
   我可以吃一口嗎？

5. He is used to eating out all the time.
   他已經習慣時常在外面吃飯了。

6. I am supposed to go on a diet.
   我應該節食。

7. I'll skip the breakfast.
   我早餐不吃。

8. What's for breakfast?
   早餐有些什麼？

9. What would you like for lunch?
   你午餐想吃什麼？

10 I have prepared some special dishes.
   我已經做了幾道特別的菜。

11 What kind of dish is it?
   這是什麼菜？

12 Now that was a great meal.
   這頓飯真夠豐盛！

2 相關單字

營養	nutrition
胃口	appetite
口渴的	thirsty
飢餓的	starving
很餓的	hungry
飽食的	full
暴食	gluttony
貪嘴	greed
吃得過多	overfeeding

3 慣用語句

▶ veg out

發呆、無所事事、放空

說明 veg out是一句俚語，表示肉體或精神上的休息、放空一切、無須思考。

例 After a long day at work, I usually just veg out in front of the TV.

經過一整天的工作後，我經常坐在電視前面發呆休息。

例 I'm going to the mountains to veg out for a few days.

我要去山上休息一段時間什麼事都不想做。

Unit 018 早餐

土司	toast
麵包	bread
長麵包	loaf
漢堡	hamburger
三明治	sandwich (複數 sandwiches)
培根	bacon
火腿	ham
香腸	sausage
炒蛋	fried egg
水煮蛋	boiled egg
鬆餅	muffin

生活單字 萬用手冊

玉米片	cornflakes
牛奶	milk
果汁	juice
咖啡	coffee
點心	snack
果醬(有果粒)	jam
果醬(透明膠凍)	jelly

1 生活實用例句

1 What would you like for breakfast?
你早餐想吃什麼？

2 Please have another sandwich.
再吃一份三明治吧！

3 How about some coffee?
要不要喝點咖啡？

4 Would you like some coffee?
你要咖啡嗎？

5 It's snack time.
點心時間到了。

6 The milk is sour.
牛奶發酸了。

7 Would you bring us some bread?
能給我們一些麵包嗎？

8 My favorite food is hamburger.

我最喜歡的食物是漢堡。

9 They eat sandwiches for breakfast.

他們早餐吃三明治。

10 Would you buy a bottle of jam on your way home?

你回家的時候可以順便買一瓶果醬嗎？

2 相關單字

煎蛋	fried egg
炒蛋	scrambled egg
水煮蛋	boiled egg

3 慣用語句

▶ hooked

深深著迷

說明 hook 字面意思是「鉤住」、「掛起」的意思，可以藉此引申為男女關係之間的「著迷」意思。

例 I really like Tina, my new girlfriend. After just two dates, I'm hooked!

我真的很喜歡我的新女友蒂娜。約會過兩次後，我就被她深深吸引了。

Unit 019　餐點

菜餚	cuisine
開胃菜	appetizer
沙拉	salad
(沙拉的)醬汁	dressing
湯	soup
主菜	entrée
主菜	main dish
餐點	course
肉	meat
牛排	steak
豬肉	pork
火雞	turkey
鴨肉	duck
烤雞	roast chicken
排骨	chop
義大利麵	spaghetti
海鮮	seafood
魚	fish
蝦	shrimp
螃蟹	crab
小菜	side dish

甜點	dessert
宵夜	midnight snack
剩菜	leftover

1
生活實用例句

1 I haven't tasted meat for ages.
我已有好久沒吃肉了。

2 I'll have a sirloin steak, medium.
我要沙朗牛排,五分熟。

3 The soup is ready.
湯好了。

4 I want some too, please.
我也要(吃)一些。

5 I'd like to order wine.
我想要點葡萄酒。

6 Coffee would be fine.
咖啡就可以了。

7 I'd like a salad.
我要(點)沙拉!

2
相關單字

蔬菜湯	vegetable soup
洋蔥湯	onion soup

Unit 020　蔬菜

蔬菜	vegetables
洋芋	potato （複數 potatoes）
紅蘿蔔	carrot
洋蔥	onion
甜菜	beet
包心菜	cabbage
花椰菜	cauliflower
芹菜	celery
萵苣	lettuce
菠菜	spinach
南瓜	pumpkin
玉米	corn
豌豆	pea
竹筍	bamboo
茄子	eggplant
蕃茄	tomato （複數 tomatoes）
香菇	mushroom
蘆筍	asparagus
大蒜	garlic
青蔥	green onion

水果

水果	fruit
蘋果	apple
梨子	pear
李子	plum
香橙	orange
桃子	peach (複數 peaches)
葡萄柚	grapefruit
檸檬	lemon
萊姆	lime
番石榴	guava
櫻桃	cherry (複數 cherries)
葡萄	grape
草莓	strawberry (複數 strawberries)
橄欖	olive
奇異果	kiwi
木瓜	papaya
椰子	coconut
甜瓜	cantaloupe
鳳梨	pineapple
香蕉	banana

Unit 022　烘焙

烘焙	bake
麵粉	flour
發酵粉	baking powder
蘇打	soda
奶油	butter
奶酪	cheese
果醬	jam
蘋果醬	apple butter
花生醬	peanut butter
美乃滋	mayonnaise
人造黃油	margarine
蜂蜜	honey
巧克力	chocolate
堅果	nut
葡萄乾	raisin
花生	peanut
可可粉	cocoa powder
香草精	vanilla extract
糖	sugar
方糖	lump sugar

Unit 023 點心、零食

甜點	dessert
零食	snacks
小餅乾	cookie
小麵包	biscuit
蛋糕	cake
糖果	candy (複數 candies)
熱狗	hot dog
香蕉船	banana split
甜甜圈	doughnut
披薩	pizza
派	pie
葡萄乾	raisin
洋蔥圈	onion ring
炸花枝圈	fried calamari
潛水艇堡	submarine sandwich
爆米花	popcorn
洋芋片	potato chips
優格	yogurt
冰淇淋	ice cream

甜筒	ice cream cone
冰棒	Popsicle
巧克力	chocolate
聖代	sundae
布丁	pudding

1 生活實用例句

1 We grow a lot of different vegetables.

我們種植多種不同的蔬菜。

2 We can crack nuts in the nutcrackers.

我們可以把堅果放在胡桃鉗裡軋碎。

3 I'd like a little ice cream.

我要來一點冰淇淋。

4 The child is eating a tub of ice cream.

孩子在吃冰淇淋。

5 Who wants an ice cream cone?

誰要吃甜筒？

6 I dropped some ice cream on the floor.

我把冰淇淋滴到地上了。

2 相關單字

一球冰淇淋	a tub of ice cream
冷凍優格	frozen yogurt

Unit 024 飲料

喝(飲料)	drink
冷飲	cold drinks
飲料	beverage
水	water
礦泉水	mineral water
氣泡式礦泉水	sparkling water
酒	liqueurs
酒精飲料	alcohol
咖啡	coffee
茶	tea
淡茶	weak tea
濃茶	strong tea
紅茶	black tea
冰紅茶	iced black tea
奶昔	shake

巧克力奶昔	chocolate shake
果汁	juice
蘋果汁	apple juice
柳橙汁	orange juice
檸檬汁	lemonade
(味道、氣味)濃的	strong

Unit 025 咖啡

咖啡	coffee
冰咖啡	iced coffee
黑咖啡	black coffee
濃縮咖啡	Espresso
拿鐵	Latte
卡布其諾	Cappuccino
摩卡咖啡	Mocha
巴西咖啡	Brazilian
曼特寧咖啡	Mendeling
爪哇咖啡	Java
藍山咖啡	Blue Mountain
滴漏式咖啡	drip coffee
即溶咖啡	instant coffee
咖啡因	caffeine

低咖啡因咖啡	decaf
一杯咖啡	a cup of coffee

1 相關單字

咖啡研磨機	coffee grinder
咖啡機	coffeemaker
咖啡壺	coffeepot
咖啡渣	coffee grounds
奶油球	creamer
糖包	sugar

Unit 026　酒精飲料

葡萄酒	wine
紅酒	red wine
白葡萄酒	pale wine
白酒	white wine
白蘭地	brandy
啤酒、一杯啤酒	beer
淡啤酒	light beer
黑啤酒	dark beer
生啤酒	draft beer

麥酒	ale
烈酒	spirit
威士忌	whiskey
伏特加	vodka
馬丁尼酒	martini
蘋果酒	cider
香檳酒	champagne
雞尾酒	cocktail

1

生活實用例句

1 May I help you to another glass of wine?

我再來幫你斟杯酒好嗎?

2 Brandy is a strong liquor.

白蘭地是一種烈酒。

3 I am drunk.

我醉了。

4 He had a terrible hangover after the New Year's Eve party.

在除夕夜的派對後,他宿醉得十分難受。

5 Buy me a beer, Daniel.

丹尼爾,幫我買杯啤酒。

2 相關單字

酒醉的、酒鬼	drunk
酒後開車	drunk-driving
宿醉	hangover
微醉的	tipsy

Unit 027 料理配方

配方	recipe
食譜、菜單	menu
加調味料	season
調味料、調味	flavor
味道	taste
(沙拉的)醬料	dressing
香草	herbs
添加	add
撒、撒在面上的屑狀物	sprinkle
油	oil
植物油	vegetable oil
橄欖油	olive oil
麵粉	flour

澱粉	starch
太白粉	corn starch
地瓜粉	sweet potato starch

1 生活實用例句

1 What is the recipe?
這是什麼配方？

2 This is a special recipe from Japan.
這是來自日本的特殊食譜。

3 What's on the menu today?
今天有什麼餐點？

4 You can use fresh herbs to flavor the soup.
你可以在湯裡加香草來調味。

5 Could you tell me what's in this?
你能告訴我這種食品有哪些成分嗎？

2 相關單字

油膩的	oily
(烤雞等用的)填料	dressing

3 慣用語句

▶ add fuel to the fire

火上添油

說明 這是一句俚語用法，fuel 是「燃料」、「汽油」，字面意思是將汽油加到火焰中，引申為中文「火上添油」。也可以是 add fuel to the flames 的說法。

例 Stop saying it. Are you trying to add fuel to the fire?

不要再說了！你是要火上添油嗎？

Unit 028 調味料、醬料

加調味、調味料	flavor
香料	spice
鹽	salt
糖	sugar
味精	monosodium glutamate
醬油	soy sauce
麻油	sesame seed oil

醋	vinegar
蔥	spring onion
薑	ginger
蒜	garlic
紅辣椒	red pepper
黑胡椒	black pepper
醬汁	sauce
牛排醬	steak sauce
烤肉汁	barbecue sauce
蕃茄醬	ketchup
塔巴斯科辣調味汁	Tabasco
芥末	mustard
醃汁	pickle
辣椒粉	chili powder
桂香	cinnamon
小茴香	cumin
丁香	clove
咖哩粉	curry

1

生活實用例句

1 I think we should add more wine.
　　我認為應該多加點酒。

2 Remember to add a touch of salt.
　　記得要加一點鹽。

3 We need to add some spices to the soup.

這道湯需要加一些香料。

4 I think we should add more soy sauce to this dish.

我覺得這道菜應該要多加點醬油。

5 She flavored the meat with onion.

她在肉裡加洋蔥調味。

6 The sauce is flavored with pepper.

醬汁裡加了胡椒調味。

7 I will marinate this in teriyaki sauce.

我會用照燒醬來醃。

2 相關單字

少許	a touch of
少許的鹽	a touch of salt
撒少許的糖	sprinkle with a touch of sugar
把魚泡在鹽水中	pickle the fish in brine
把蝦子泡在鹽水	brine the shrimp
把肉裹上麵粉	coat the meat with the flour
擠少許的檸檬汁	squeeze a bit of lemon juice

Unit 029 調理食材

切、割	cut
切丁	dice
切片	slice
切絲	shred
刨絲	grate
剁(肉)	chop
剝皮	peel
磨成粉狀	grind
擠壓	squeeze
過濾	strain
涼拌	blend
糖醋	sweet and sour
醃漬	pickle
用滷汁浸泡	marinade
用濃鹽水浸泡	brine
裹上、塗抹	coat
打(蛋)	beat (an egg)

1 生活實用例句

1. How should I cook these steaks?
   我該怎麼煎這些牛排？
2. Be careful not to cut your hand.
   小心不要切到手。
3. I'll cut the lettuce and other vegetables.
   我要切萵苣和其他蔬菜。
4. Why don't you peel and dice the carrots for me?
   你何不幫我把馬鈴薯削皮、切丁？
5. He squeezed some juice from a lemon.
   他從檸檬擠出了一些汁。

2 相關單字

小火煮	cook on low heat
中火煮	cook on medium heat
大火煮	cook on high heat
做飯	fix a meal
做沙拉	fix a salad
擠少許的檸檬汁	squeeze a bit of lemon juice

3 慣用語句

▶ squeeze a bit of lemon juice
擠少許的檸檬汁

說明 squeeze 是「擠壓」的意思,像是擠檸檬、青春痘、牙膏等都適用喔!

衍生 squeezer 擠壓器

例 I cut the lemon in half and squeeze the juice into the bowl.

我把檸檬切半,然後擠(檸檬)汁液進碗裡。

Unit 030 烹調

烹煮	cook
(在架上)燒烤	grill
(在爐內)燒烤	roast
焗烤	gratin
燒、烤	broil
烘焙(麵包等)	bake
烤(土司等)	toast
油炸、油煎	fry

油炸	deep-fry
淺鍋油炸	pan-fry
快炒	stir-fry
嫩煎	saute
沸煮	boil
中火慢煮、燉	simmer
蒸	steam
燙煮	blanch
水煮	poach
以文火悶煮	braise
燴、燉、燜	stew
煙燻	smoke
微波加熱	nuke

1
生活實用例句

1 Do you think this soup is OK?
你覺得這個湯可以嗎？

2 Nuke it for 2 minutes.
微波加熱兩分鐘。

3 Don't overcook the chicken.
不要把雞肉烤得太熟。

4 Did you burn it?
你把它烤焦了嗎？

生活單字 萬用手冊

2 相關單字

加熱	heat up
炊具	cooker
料理、烹調	cooking
煮得太熟	overcooked
(牛排)全熟	well done
(牛排)七分熟	medium well
(牛排)五分熟	medium
(牛排)三分熟	medium rare
(牛排)一分熟、不熟的	rare

Unit 031 口味

美味的	delicious
色香味俱佳	savory
難吃	yucky
好吃	yum
酸的	sour
(水果的)酸的	tart
醋酸的	vinegary
甜的	sweet

苦的	bitter
辛辣的	spicy
辣的	hot
鹹的	salty
清淡的	light
(食物等)清淡的	plain
水分充足	watery
乾乾的	dry
油膩的	rich
(佐料)過多的	heavy
嫩的、軟的	tender
咬不動的	tough
酥脆的	crispy
酥脆的、鮮嫩的	crisp

生 活 實 用 例 句

1 It's very delicious.
這非常美味。

2 The meat tastes delicious.
這肉味道真好。

3 It's yucky.
好難吃！

4 It's tasteless.

沒味道。

5 This chocolate cake is too rich for me.

這個巧克力蛋糕對我來説太濃了。

6 The celery is fresh and crisp.

這芹菜新鮮脆嫩。

7 He only eats lean meat.

他只吃瘦肉。

8 It's too rare.

它太生了。

9 This meat is overcooked.

這肉煮得太老了。

2 相關單字

入味的	full-bodied
燒焦的	burnt
沒味道的	tasteless
未煮熟的	raw
腐壞的	rotten
臭味的	stinking

3 慣用語句

▶ eat another bite
吃不下、飽了

說明 bite 是「咬一口」的意思，couldn't eat another bite 字面意思是「再也吞不下另一口了」，引申為「吃不下」、「飽了」的意思。

例 A：How about some sandwiches?
要不要吃一些三明治？

B：No, thanks. I couldn't eat another bite.
不用了，謝謝！我實在是吃不下了！

Unit 032　廚房、飯廳用具

廚房用具	kitchenware
爐子	stove
瓦斯爐	gas stove
微波爐	microwave
冰箱	refrigerator
冷凍庫	freezer
烤箱	oven

電鍋	electric rice cooker
熱水瓶	thermos
抽風機	exhaust fan
抽油煙機	range hood
通風機	ventilator
餐桌	dining table
桌布	tablecloth
餐椅	dining chair
餐具架	sideboard
餐具櫃	cupboard
餐盤架	plate rack
餐巾	napkin
拖盤	tray

1

生 活 實 用 例 句

1 Do you know how to use the microwave?

你知道怎麼使用微波爐嗎？

2 Tom reached into the refrigerator and pulled out a beer.

湯姆把手伸進冰箱，拿出一罐啤酒。

3 She took the pie out of the oven and turned the gas off.

她將派從烤箱中拿出來並關掉了瓦斯。

4 Ben spread the tablecloth and set the table for dinner.

班舖上桌布擺好餐具準備開飯。

5 She handed him a napkin.

她遞給他一條餐巾。

2 慣用語句

▶ dine out

外出用餐

說明 正式用法,表示出外到餐廳用餐。

衍生 diner 【主美】路邊賣簡餐餐廳

例 We rarely dine out these days.

這些日子以來我們很少出外用餐。

Unit 033 烹調餐具

菜刀	kitchen knife
中式菜刀	cleaver
砧板	cutting board
鍋	pot
平底鍋	pan
湯鍋	soup pan

鍋鏟	turner
抹刀、刮刀	spatula
大湯匙	soupspoon
攪拌機	mixer
攪拌器	beater
打蛋器	eggbeater
攪拌器	stirrer
濾器、濾鍋	colander
磨碎機	grater
榨汁機	squeezer
檸檬擠壓器	lemon squeezer
開瓶器	bottle opener
開罐器	can opener
削皮器	peeler
馬鈴薯削皮器	potato peeler
過濾器	strainer
食物處理機	food processor
果汁機	blender
冰淇淋杓子	ice cream scoop
量杯	measuring cup
烤肉叉	spit
撖麵棍	rolling pin

1 生活實用例句

1 There's plenty of cupboard space in the kitchen for all your pots and pans.

廚房裡有很多碗櫃的空間可以放你的鍋碗瓢盆。

2 Did you see my vegetable peeler?

你有看見我的蔬菜削皮刀嗎？

3 Have you got a lemon squeezer?

你有擠檸檬器嗎？

2 相關單字

保鮮膜	foil
鋁箔紙	aluminum foil
保鮮盒	preserving box
咖啡壺	coffee pot
茶壺	teapot
油炸鍋	frying pan

3 慣用語句

▶ grub

（簡單的）食物

說明 非正式用法，表示「簡單的食品」，類似用法還有 chow。

例 The grub they serve in the cafeteria is pretty good!

這間咖啡店提供的簡餐還不錯。

Unit 034　餐具

器皿	utensil
銀餐具	silverware
餐具	cutlery
餐刀	knife
牛排刀	steak knife
叉子	fork
碗	bowl
筷子	chopsticks
盤子	dish
湯匙	spoon
長柄杓、湯杓	ladle

大湯匙	tablespoon
小調羹	teaspoon
瓶子	bottle
咖啡壺	coffeepot
咖啡杯	coffee cup
杯子	cup
水杯	glass
酒杯	wineglass
茶壺	teapot
壺、罐	pitcher

生活實用例句

1 This store sells cooking utensils.
這間商店有出售炊具。

2 My silverware was stolen last night.
昨晚我的銀器被偷走了。

3 Would you please change a new knife for me?
可以幫我換一支新的刀子嗎？

4 I prefer to use a knife and fork.
我偏好使用刀叉。

5 I eat a bowl of cereal every morning.
我每天早上吃一碗麥片。

6 Who's going to do the dishes?
誰要洗碗？

7 Would you like a cup of coffee?
你要喝杯咖啡嗎？

8 May I have a glass of water?
我可以喝一杯水？

2 相關單字

主菜叉子	dinner fork
沙拉叉子	salad fork
調味碟子	saucer
胡椒罐	pepper shaker
鹽罐	salt shaker
醬碟	saucer
包刀	bread knife
奶油刀	butter knife
湯碗	soup bowl
沙拉碗	salad bowl
牙籤	toothpick

3 慣用語句

▶ do the dishes

洗碗

說明 「洗碗」不必用 wash，只要 do the dishes 就可以。記得 dishes 要用複數形式。

衍生 dishwasher 洗碗機

例 I'll do the dishes tonight, honey.
親愛的，今晚由我來洗碗。

Unit 035 速食

速食	fast food
垃圾食物	junk food
菜單	menu
點餐	order
漢堡	hamburger
炸雞	fried chicken
雞塊	chicken nuggets
薯條	French fries
熱狗	hot dog
汽水	soft drink

爆米花	popcorn
可樂	Cola
可口可樂	Coke
百事可樂	Pepsi
咖啡	coffee
奶精	cream
糖包	sugar
大杯(飲料)	large
小杯(飲料)	small
蕃茄醬	ketchup
芥末醬	mustard

生活實用例句

1 You should stop eating so much junk food.
你應該停止吃這麼多的垃圾食物。

2 What do you want? Coffee or tea?
你要什麼？咖啡或茶？

3 Pass me the ketchup, please.
遞蕃茄醬給我！

4 Stop eating the French fries.
別再吃薯條了！

5 I put a dash of mustard on the hot dogs.

我在熱狗上放了少量的芥末。

6 Would you like some sugar for your coffee?

你的咖啡要加糖嗎？

7 Do you take cream in your coffee?

你的咖啡裡要加奶精嗎？

8 I'd like some popcorn and some fries, please.

我要一些爆米花和薯條。

9 I'll have a large cola, no ice.

我要一杯大杯的可樂，不要冰塊。

2 相關單字

小杯可樂	a small Cola
大杯可樂	a large Cola
吸管	straw
紙巾	paper napkins
拖盤	tray
紙杯	paper cup
麥當勞	McDonald's
肯德基	Kentucky Fried Chicken

3 慣用語句

▶ junk food
垃圾食物

說明 junk food 是垃圾食物，而投遞到信箱中的廣告信函就叫做 junk mail，至於電子郵件中常收到的垃圾信件，則是 spam。

例 There's a letter for you and the rest is junk mail.

有一封你的信，其餘的都是垃圾郵件。

Unit 036 超市

超市	supermarket
購物手推車	shopping cart
提籃	basket
磅秤	scale
區域	section
置物架	shelf
走道	aisle
冷凍食品	frozen foods
肉類	meat

海鮮類	seafood
蔬菜類	vegetable
素食	vegetable diet
水果	fruit
烘烤食品	bakery
穀類	cereal
乳製品	dairy
罐頭食品	canned goods

1 生活實用例句

1 I have to stop at the supermarket on the way home.
我要在回家的路上順道去超市。

2 We buy milk at the dairy.
我們在乳品店買牛奶。

3 Where can I find a shopping cart?
我可以在哪裡找到購物推車？

2 相關單字

詢問櫃台	information counter
結帳櫃台	checkout counter
現金結帳通道	cash lane
收銀處	cash desk

3 慣用語句

▶ pump iron

舉重

說明 pump 是抽水的意思，pump iron 是
形容一次又一次舉起「鐵器」的動
作，也就引申為「舉重」之意。

例 Let's go to the gym and pump some iron.

我們去健身房練舉重吧！

Unit 037 計量單位

數量	quantity
一袋豆子	a bag of beans
一束花	a bouquet of flowers
一束玫瑰	a bouquet of roses
一箱蘋果	a box of apples
一串葡萄	a bunch of grapes
一串鑰匙	a bunch of keys
一塊條型巧克力	a bar of chocolate
一罐起司	a can of cheese

一瓶蕃茄醬	a bottle of ketchup
一盒菸	a carton of cigarettes
一桶啤酒	a tub of beer
一球冰淇淋	a tub of ice cream
一打的蛋	a dozen of eggs
一條麵包	a loaf of bread
一盒柳橙汁	a carton of orange juice
兩條麵包	two loaves of bread
一段口香糖	a stick of chewing gum
一串香蕉	a hand of bananas
一杯水	a glass of water
一點鹽	a touch of salt
微量的鹽	a tad of salt
少量的醋	a dash of vinegar
一點檸檬	a bit of lemon
一片派	a piece of the pie
一捲壁紙	a piece of wallpaper
一張紙	a piece of paper
一張紙	a sheet of paper
兩張紙	two sheets of paper
一件珠寶	a piece of jewellery
一把剪刀	a pair of scissors

一個圓規	a pair of compasses
一盎司的巧克力脆片	an ounce of chocolate chips
一公升的酒	a liter of wine
一夸脫的油	a quart of oil
一加侖的牛奶	a gallon of milk
一磅的砂糖	a pound of sugar
一瓣大蒜	a clove of garlic
一團毛線	a ball of wool

1 生 活 實 用 例 句

1. Could you give me a piece of paper?
   你能給我一張紙嗎？

2. The pianist played a piece by Chopin.
   鋼琴家演奏了一曲蕭邦的作品。

3. I had a can of soup for lunch.
   我午餐吃了一罐湯。

4. Get a loaf of white bread from the corner store.
   去轉角的商店買一條白麵包回來。

5. This recipe makes three dozen cookies.
   這道食譜需要三打的餅乾。

6 My mother brought home a box of chocolates.

我母親帶一盒巧克力回家。

7 He ate a whole box of chocolates.

他吃掉一整盒巧克力。

8 There are 16 ounces in one pound.

一磅要 16 盎司。

9 Would you buy me a carton of milk?

可以幫我買一盒牛奶嗎？

2 相關單字

一半	half
許多的(形容可數名詞)	many
許多的(形容不可數名詞)	much
很少的(形容可數名詞)	few
不多的(形容不可數名詞)	little

3 慣用語句

說明 dozen 是計量單位，表示「一打」（12個），至於「6個」則可以用 half a dozen 表示。注意，dozen 前面加數字時不必加 s。

例 Could you get me half a dozen eggs when you go to the shop?

你去商店的時候可以幫我買半打的蛋嗎？

Unit 038　正式服裝

【總稱】衣服	clothing
衣服	clothes
服裝	costume
正式服裝	dress
禮服	formal dress
燕尾服	tailcoat
夜禮服	evening dress
燕尾服、晚禮服	dress suit
無燕尾晚禮服	tuxedo
長袍禮服	robe
長袍	tunic
大衣	coat
輕便大衣	topcoat
短夾克	bomber jacket
斗篷	cloak
外衣	outerwear
外套	jacket
風衣	dust coat
風衣	outer coat
雨衣	raincoat

1

生活實用例句

1 I've got all these clothes that I never wear.

這些衣服都是我從未穿過的。

2 He changed his costume for the party.

他換了衣服去參加派對。

3 Liz wore a black dress to the party.

麗茲穿了一件黑色洋裝參加派對。

4 Put on your coat, David.

大衛，穿上你的大衣。

5 The keys are in my jacket pocket.

鑰匙在我的外套口袋裡。

6 My mother bought me an outer coat.

我的母親買給我一件風衣。

7 I forgot to take my raincoat.

我忘記帶雨衣了！

2 慣用語句

▶ put on
穿上(衣服)、擦上（化妝品）

說明 put on 是表示「穿上」的動作，而 wear 則表示「穿著衣服」的事實。

例 Put your shoes on.
穿上你的鞋子。

例 She's wearing a gold ring.
她戴著一只金戒指。

Unit 039 家居服

休閒服	casual clothes
便裝	ordinary clothes
短袖圓領衫	T-shirt
上衣	tops
工作服	overall
連身衣褲	jumpsuit
牛仔裝	jeans
牛仔褲	jeans-pants
水手衫	middy blouse
馬球衫	polo shirt
網衫	mesh shirt
運動短褲	trunks
無袖背心	tank top
無袖上衣	sleeveless top
無袖衫	sleeveless tee
短運動褲	shorts
背心	vest

1 生活實用例句

1. He wore a T-shirt and jeans.
   他穿了一件 T 恤和牛仔衣。

2. I'm looking for a matching top to go with this skirt.
   我在找一件可以搭配這件裙子的上衣。

3. I never wear jeans for work.
   我上班時從不穿牛仔衣。

4. I wore the black dress with the short sleeves.
   我穿著黑色無袖洋裝。

5. My grandfather always wore his vest buttoned up.
   我爺爺總是會穿著他扣好的背心。

2 慣用語句

▶ slip-on
便於穿脫

說明 slip-on 可當名詞或形容詞使用，表示「便於穿脫」，slip 是「滑入」的意思，套用在衣物或鞋子上就是「方便穿脫」的意思。

例 I bought a pair of slip-ons.
我買了一雙便鞋。

例 I can't find my slip-on shoes.
我找不到我的便鞋。

Unit 040 男性服裝

男長禮服	frock coat
男裝	suit
男裝	menswear
西裝	business suit
雙排扣西裝	double-breasted jacket
襯衫	shirt
(男用)襯衫式長睡衣	nightshirt
褲子	pants
皮帶	belt
寬鬆的長褲	slacks
領帶	tie
領帶夾	tie clip
領帶別針	tie tack
蝴蝶結領帶	bow tie
皮鞋	leather shoes

1 生活實用例句

1 I picked out a black suit.
   我挑了一套黑色西裝。

2 I need a new pair of gray pants to go with this jacket.
   我需要買一件灰色褲子搭配外套。

3 They both wore gray slacks and white shirts.
   他們兩人都穿灰色寬鬆褲子搭配襯衫。

4 I want to buy a silk tie for my husband.
   我想要幫我先生買一件絲質領帶。

5 That is knotted like a bow.
   那被打成蝴蝶結領帶。

6 Where did you buy this tie clip?
   你在哪裡買的領帶夾？

2 相關單字

男性	man (複數men)
紳士	gentleman (複數gentlemen)
男孩	boy

3 慣用語句

▶ tie
平手

說明 tie 除了是名詞「領帶」，也可以當成動詞「打結」使用。而另一個解釋則為「平手」。

應用 tie a knot / necktie 　打個結/領帶

tie up one's shoelace 打鞋帶

例 The score is tied (up) at 3 to 3.

比賽三比三平手。

Unit 041　女性服裝

女西裝	tailored suit
女用襯衫	blouse
洋裝	dress
結婚禮服	wedding dress
新娘禮服	bridal gown
孕婦裝	pregnant dress
裙子	skirt
迷你裙	miniskirt
窄裙	slim skirt

一字裙	wrap skirt
熱褲	hot-pants
女燈籠褲	bloomer
女睡袍	gown
女睡衣	nightdress
襯褲	underpants
襯裙	petticoat
連襪褲	panty hose

1 相關單字

1. Liz wore a sleeveless blouse.
   麗茲穿著一件無袖上衣。
2. I need to buy a short dress.
   我需要買一件短裙！
3. The little girl was dressed in a very short skirt.
   小女孩穿了一條很短的裙子。

2 相關單字

女性	woman (複數women)
女士	lady (複數ladies)
女孩	girl
胸罩	bra

| 胸罩尺寸 | bra size |
| 胸罩罩杯 | bra cup size |

3 慣用語句

▶ birthday suit

裸體

說明 口語化用法，來源是「出生時的穿著」，也就是光溜溜沒有穿衣物！

例 He walked out of the bathroom in his birthday suit.

他沒有穿衣服就走出浴室了。

Unit 042 特殊服裝

全套衣裝	outfit
制服	uniform
初生嬰兒的全套用品	layette
尿布	diaper
紙尿布	disposable diaper
兔寶寶裝	romper
童裝	children's wear
兒童燈籠短褲	knickers

燈籠褲	knickerbockers
羽絨衣	down jacket
浴衣	bathrobe
泳衣	swimwear
游泳衣褲	swimsuit
游泳褲	bathing trunks
游泳衣	bathing suit
比基尼泳衣	bikini
緊身衣	tights
塑身衣	shaper
圍裙	apron
(有護胸的)圍裙	pinafore

生活實用例句

1 Susan wore a black outfit.
蘇珊穿了一件黑色套裝。

2 I saw a soldier in uniform lying down there.
我看見一個穿制服的士兵躺在那裡！

3 Buy two boxes of disposable diapers on your way home.
你回家的時候，要買兩盒拋棄式尿布。

4 The goose down quilts are on sale today in this store
今天這家商店裡的羽絨被特價中。

5　Did you see my bathrobe?
　　你有看見我的浴衣嗎？

6　I forgot to bring my bikini top.
　　我忘記帶我的比基尼上衣。

7　Remember to bring my swimsuit.
　　記得帶泳衣給我！

2 相關單字

學校制服	school uniform
嬰兒鞋	baby shoes
嬰兒學步鞋	toddler's learning shoes
兒童套裝	children's suits
兒童短褲	children's shorts
高爾夫球褲	plus fours

3 慣用語句

▶ bikini line
比基尼線

說明　女性穿著比基尼泳裝時，下半身的泳裝在大腿與腹部交接處就稱為 bikini line。通常這個地方是要特別保養，不能出現任何毛髮，以免有礙觀瞻。

Unit 043 飾品

飾品	accessory
珠寶	jewelry
珍珠	pearl
鑽石	diamond
黃金	gold
14K 金	14K gold
胸針	brooch
胸花	corsage
袖扣	cuff link
別針	pin
耳環	earring
項鍊	necklace
手鐲	bracelet
戒指	ring
腳鍊	anklet

1
生活實用例句

1 Sunglasses are much more than a fashion accessory.

太陽眼鏡不只是配件而已！

2 There is a piece of silver jewelry on the desk.

桌上有一件銀飾。

3 The necklace is made of natural pearls.

這項鍊是用天然珍珠做成的。

4 This is my diamond engagement ring.

這是我的訂婚鑽戒。

5 He was wearing an earring in his left ear.

他在左耳帶著一只耳環。

6 My husband bought me a pearl necklace.

我先生送我一付珍珠項鍊。

7 She is wearing a ring set with emerald.

她戴著一枚嵌有祖母綠的戒指。

2 相關單字

玉、翡翠	jade
紅寶石	carbuncle
紅玉髓	carnelian
藍寶石	sapphire
祖母綠	emerald
血石髓	blood stone
紅條紋瑪瑙	sardonyx
蛋白石	opal
橄欖石	peridot
月光石	moon stone
水晶	crystal
黃水晶	yellow quartz
紫水晶	amethyst
碧璽	tourmaline
石榴石	garnet

3 慣用語句

▶ wear
穿戴（珠寶）、擦上（香水）

說明 wear除了表示穿上衣物之外，也可以表示「穿戴珠寶（眼鏡、假髮）」或是「擦上香水」的意思。

相關 put on  穿上(衣物)

例 He wears glasses for reading.
他戴眼鏡看書。

例 Did you wear perfume?
你有擦香水嗎？

Unit 044 內衣、睡衣

【總稱】內衣	underwear
晨衣、睡袍	gown
(男子、小孩的)汗衫	undershirt
四角褲	boxer shorts
三角褲(男女適穿)	brief
短內褲	panties
燈籠褲	knickers
長內衣褲	long johns
束腹	corset
緊身內衣	corselet
一件式緊身衣	body stocking
緊身(男)上衣	body shirt
【美】女式緊身衣褲	body suit
睡衣	pajamas
長睡衣	nightshirt

1
生活實用例句

1 She had removed her underwear.
   她脫掉了內衣。

2 He just got up and was still in pajamas.
   他才剛剛起床，還穿著睡衣。

2
慣用語句

▶ **tightie whities**
   緊身小內褲

說明 俚語用法，指男用貼身的緊身小內褲。

相異 boxer shorts 寬鬆大內褲

例 Which do you prefer, tightie whities or boxer shorts?

你喜歡哪一個？緊身內褲或是寬鬆大內褲？

Unit 045 修改服飾

編織	knit
脫線	loose thread
修理、修補、縫補	mend
拼布	patch
調整	adjust
縫紉機	sewing machine
縫紉線	thread
縫製(衣服)	tailor
修改衣物	tailoring
接縫處	seam
縫衣針	needle
別針	pin
刺繡、給…加上裝飾	embroider
刺繡(法)	embroidery
鉤針編織	crochet
鉤針	crochet needle

1 相關單字

(給上衣)縫上扣子	sew a button on (the coat)
縫補上衣	mend a coat
用線縫	sew with thread
拼製成一條被子	patch a quilt
修改褲子的長度	adjust the pants length

2 慣用語句

▶ a ball of wool
一球的毛線

說明 ball 是「球」的意思也有「球狀體」的意思，而毛線捲起來一團一團的，是不是很像一顆球呢？

例 I'm going to buy a ball of wool.
我要去買一球毛線。

例 There is a ball of string on the desk.
桌上有一團線。

Unit 046 配件

個人物品	personal item
手套	gloves
面紗	veil
頭巾	knitted shawl
頭巾	hood
領巾	cravat
披肩、圍巾	wrap
圍巾、披肩	scarf
大披巾	shawl
【口語】手帕	handkerchief
手帕	hankie
頭飾	headdress
頭巾	turban
耳罩、耳套	earmuffs
眼鏡	glasses
太陽眼鏡	sun glasses
隱形眼鏡	contact lens
手錶	watch (複數 watches)
雨傘	umbrella
(女用)陽傘	shade

小型手提箱	briefcase
袋子	bag
有肩帶的皮包	shoulder bag
背包	backpack
錢包	purse
皮夾	wallet
(女用)手提包	handbag
背包	knapsack
手提箱	suitcase
放套裝的手提箱	suiter
附輪子的手提箱	wheeled suiter

1

生活實用例句

1 Remember to wear your gloves.
   記得要戴手套。

2 My boyfriend bought me a wrap as
   a birthday present.
   我男朋友送給我一條圍巾當生日禮物。

3 I felt a few spots of rain so I put my
   umbrella up.
   我有感覺到雨點，所以我撐起了傘。

4 I can't find my bag.
   我找不到我的袋子。

5 I left my wallet in a cab.

我把錢包遺忘在計程車裡了！

 **2 相關單字**

露指長手套	mittens
烤箱手套	oven glove
棒球手套	baseball glove
拳擊手套	boxing glove
摺疊傘	a folding umbrella

3 慣用語句

▶ **wrap**

圍繞、披上

說明 wrap 除了是表示「圍巾」、「披肩」之外，也是動詞「圍繞」或「披上」的意思。

類似 tie（名詞）領帶、（動詞）打領帶

例 She wrapped a scarf around her neck.

她把圍巾圍在脖子上。

Unit 047 鞋、襪

【總稱】鞋襪	footwear=footgear
襪類	hosiery
短襪	socks
長襪	stockings
長統襪	high socks
網眼長統襪	fishnet stockings
(齊膝的)半長筒襪	knee-socks
絲襪	silk stockings
鞋子	shoes
女高跟鞋	high heel shoes
低跟平底鞋	low heel shoes
皮鞋	leather shoes
休閒鞋	casual shoes
運動鞋	sports shoes
跑步鞋	running shoes
網球鞋	tennis shoes
橡皮底帆布鞋	sneaker
平底鞋	flattie
靴子	boots
馬靴	jackboots
橡膠高統套鞋	rubber boots

拖鞋	slippers
涼鞋	sandals
木屐	clogs
平底夾腳鞋、人字拖	thong
便鞋(無帶扣)	slip-on

1 相關單字

鞋帶	shoelaces
(鞋帶等)繫緊	tie
鞋底	sole
鞋後跟	heel
鞋油	shoe polish
鞋拔	shoehorn
鞋架	shoe rack
鞋匠	shoemaker
補鞋匠	cobbler

2 慣用語句

▶ a pair of socks

一雙短襪

說明 因為襪子都是兩隻，所以計量單位是以 pair（一雙）為主。

類似 a pair of slip-ons 一雙便鞋

例 I bought a pair of black socks last night.

我昨晚買了一雙黑色短襪。

Unit 048 穿/脫服裝

穿著	wear
穿上、戴上	take on
脫下	take off
脫去(衣服)	strip
穿衣、更衣	dress
脫去(衣服、裝飾)	undress
(外出時)更衣	dress oneself
扣住(帶扣、扣子)	buckle
解開(帶扣、扣子)	unbuckle
扣上扣子	button
解開扣子	unbutton
打上(領帶等)	tie
脫掉領帶	untie
拉上拉鏈	zip
拉開拉鏈	unzip

1 相關單字

穿外套	wear a coat
穿靴子	wear boots
圍圍巾	wear a scarf
抹香水	wear perfume
常穿著、戴著	have...in wear
在某人的手帕上打個結	tie a knot in one's handkerchief
打領帶	tie a necktie
給某人繫上圍裙	tie an apron round sb.
結鞋帶	tie up one's shoelace
扣上鈕釦	button up
穿上盛裝、精心打扮	dress up

2 慣用語句

▶ button up
扣上

說明 button 除了是名詞「扣子」之外，也可以當成動詞「扣上扣子」使用。button up 為常用片語。

例 Button up your coat, OK? It's cold out.
扣上外套的扣子好嗎？外面很冷。

丈量	measure
尺寸	size
三圍	measurements
衣領	neck
袖子	sleeve
袖長	sleeve length
褲長	pants length
女性胸圍	bust
男性胸圍	chest
腰圍	waist
臀圍	hip
合身	fit
適合	suit
非常合身	perfect fit
大的	big
比較大的	bigger
小的	small
比較小的	smaller
寬的	wide
比較寬的	wider
寬鬆的	loose

比較鬆的	looser
鬆垮的	baggy
長度	length
長的	long
比較長的	longer
短的	short
比較短的	shorter
緊的	tight
比較緊的	tighter

1 相關單字

變長	lengthen
縮短	shorten
超小號	extra small(縮寫 XS)
小號	small(縮寫 S)
中號	medium(縮寫 M)
大號	large(縮寫 L)
超大號	extra large(縮寫 XL)
普通尺寸	regular
統一尺寸	free size

2 慣用語句

▶ try on
試穿（衣物）

說明 try on 是常用片語，是購買衣物前，試穿是否合身時使用。

例 A：May I try on this coat?
我可以試穿這件外套嗎？

B：Sure, go ahead.
當然可以！

Unit 050 材質

織物	fabric
(透明的、極薄的)織物	sheer
厚的	thick
厚重的	heavy
薄的	thin
舒適的	comfortable
比較舒適的	more comfortable
防水的	waterproof
不會起縐摺的	wrinkle-free
有彈性的	stretch

彈性織物	streth fabric
縫紉、縫上	sew
技藝	workmanship

1 生 活 實 用 例 句

1 How thick is the board?
這塊木板有多厚?

2 Mother used to sew me shoes.
母親過去總為我縫製鞋子。

3 These shoes are waterproof.
這些鞋子是防水的。

2 慣 用 語 句

▶ made of
由…所製成

說明 上述都是表示「由…所製成」，
made of 表示成品保留材料原來的
性質形狀，而 made from 表成品不
保留材料原來的性質形狀。

例 This chair is made of woods.
這張椅子是由木頭所製成的。

例 The wine is made from the grapes.
紅酒是由葡萄所釀製成的。

品牌	brand
搭配	match
款式	style
設計	design
流行款式	fashion
時髦的	stylish
時髦的、流行的	fashionable
新潮的	new-fashioned
保守的	conservative
暴露的	revealing
性感的	sexy
可愛的	cute
成熟的	mature
老氣	oldish
花俏的	flashy
鮮豔的	bright
顯眼的	loud
華麗的	showy
多種顏色的	colorful
獨特的	unique
現成的	ready-made

耐穿的	longwearing
耐穿的、耐磨的	wearable
(衣服)襤褸的	shabby
吸引人的	attractive
審美力	taste
(織物)極薄的	transparent
雅致的	elegant
正式的	formal
休閒的	casual

1 生 活 實 用 例 句

1 This isn't my usual brand of deodorant.

這不是我常用的除臭劑。

2 They had hundreds of styles of light in stock.

他們庫存中有好幾百種的燈品。

3 The black dress is always in style.

黑色的洋裝總是不退流行的！

4 This dress is out of style.

這件洋裝已經退流行了！

5 It's not fashionable to wear short skirts this year.

今年不流行穿短裙！

2 相關單字

流行的	in general wear
最新款式	the latest design
最新款式的服飾	the latest fashion in dresses

3 慣用語句

▶ out of fashion

過時的

說明 fashion 是「流行」的意思，而「在流行之外」就是過時、不時髦的意思。一般人容易誤將 fashion 當成形容詞使用，「流行的」英文用法應為 fashionable.

相關 follow the fashion　　趕時髦

例 Don't you think this coat is out of fashion?

你不覺得這件外套退流行了嗎？

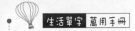

Unit 052 顏色

顏色	color
色彩豐富的	colorful
深色	dark
淺色	light
白色	white
象牙色	ivory
乳白	milk white
奶油色	crystal cream
雪白色	snowy white
青白色	bluish white
牡蠣灰	oyster white
灰色	gray
炭灰色	charcoal gray
煙灰色	smoky gray
霧灰色	misty gray
淡灰	light gray
灰泥色	gray-marl
藍灰	blue gray
深灰	dark gray
銀色	silver
紅色	red

粉紅色	pink
暗粉紅	petunia pink
淡紅	reddish
淺粉紅色	baby pink
鮮粉紅色	shocking pink
玫瑰紅	rose
珊瑚紅	coral
桃紅色	peach
緋紅、猩紅	scarlet
葡萄酒紅	wine red
深紅色	crimson
紅紫色	burgundy
深紫紅色	raisin
褐紅色	maroon
棗色色	bay
巧克力色	chocolate
深紅	carmine
橙紅色	salmon pink
鮭肉色	salmon
橙色	orange
褐色	brown
淺褐色	sandy beige
芝麻色	sesame
肉色	nude
黃棕色	chamois

棕色	brown
黃褐色	tan
深褐色	dark brown
暗黃色	buff
黃土色	ocher
鐵銹色	rust brown
秋海棠色	begonia
駝色	camel
琥珀色	amber
卡其色	khaki
黃色	yellow
奶油色	cream
淡黃	canary
蛋黃	yolk yellow
深黃	deep yellow
香蕉黃	banana
黑色	black
淺黑色	light sable
金色	gold
金黃	golden yellow
米色	beige
橄欖色	olive
綠色	green
淡綠色	pale celery
翠綠	jade green

苔綠	moss green
海水綠	seaside green
青綠色	fresh green
蘋果綠	apple green
鮮綠色	emerald green
橄欖綠	olive green
竹青色	blue green
墨綠	deep green
深綠	dark green
紫銅色	purple bronze
藍色	blue
淡藍色	pale blue
淺藍色	baby blue
水藍色	blue water
天藍	sky blue
海藍色	sea blue
寶藍	royal blue
豔藍色	cobalt blue
藍黑色	blue ink
海軍藍	navy blue
土耳其藍色	turquoise blue
銀藍	sliver blue
藍綠色	aquamarine blue
靛藍	indigo blue
紫色	purple

紫羅蘭色	violet
淡紫色	orchid
淡桃紅紫	lilac
薰衣紫	lavender
深紫色	plum
淡紫色	mauve
古銅色	copper color

 慣用語句

► crystal

水晶

說明 crystal 除了是名詞「水晶」之外，更因為它清透的特色，而可以當成形容詞使用，表示「清透的」、「透明的」。

例 It's clear as crystal.

像水晶般清透。

購物

逛街採購	go shopping
隨意看看	look around
尋找(欲購商品)	look for
購買	buy
販賣	sell
出售	sale
付款	pay
貴的	expensive
便宜的	cheap
半價	half off
包裝	wrap
收據	receipt
現金	cash
付現金	pay in cash
信用卡	credit card
特價中	on sale
銷售	for sale
撿到便宜	a good deal
賣光	sell out
店員	clerk
買方	buyer

賣方	seller
暢銷書	bestseller
退款	refund

1

生活實用例句

1 Mother bought me a pair of jeans.
母親給我買了一條牛仔褲。

2 I bought a small car last week.
我上星期買了一輛小車。

3 I bought my house cheap.
這房子我買得很便宜。

4 I'm just looking around.
我只是隨意看看。

5 What are you looking for?
你有想要買什麼嗎？

6 He sold me his camera.
他把照相機賣給我。

7 J K Rowling's 'Harry Potter' novels are all bestsellers.
ＪＫ羅琳的哈利波特小說非常暢銷。

8 Is this painting for sale?
這幅畫有要出售嗎？

9 The sale of cigarettes is forbidden.
香菸是禁止販賣的。

10 The shop sold out all their shirts.

這家商店的襯衫都賣光了。

11 I'd like to pay in cash.

我要用現金付款。

2 相關單字

在模特兒身上	on the model
在銷售員身上	on the salesperson
在雜誌上	on the magazine
在型錄上	on the catalogue
在櫥窗內	in the show window
在陳列櫃中	in the showcase
試衣間	fitting room
鏡子	mirror
要求退款	demand a refund

3 慣用語句

▶ window-shopping

只看不買

說明 window shopping 原為看著櫥窗採購的意思，引申為只看不買的逛街模式。

例 Would you like to go window-shopping with us?

要不要和我們一起去逛街？

Unit 054 清洗衣物

洗潔	wash
搓揉	rub
用水清洗	rinse
(用肥皂水)浸泡	soak
髒污	dirty
乾淨	clean
洗衣精	detergent
柔軟精	softening detergent
洗衣粉	washing powder
肥皂	washing soap
漂白水	bleaching agents
漂白粉	bleaching powder
漂白劑	bleach
衣物柔軟精	fabric softener
溶解	dissolve
沖洗	flush
自助洗衣店	laundromat
洗衣店、待洗的衣物	laundry
送洗衣物籃	laundry basket
免燙處理	permanent press

使乾燥、乾的	dry
弄濕、濕的	wet
免燙的、洗好即可穿的	wash-and-wear
防水的	waterproof
不褪色的	colorfast
防縮水	shrink resistant
縮水	shrink
使褪色	fade
褪色的	faded
不褪色的	fadeless
烘乾機	dryer
洗衣機	washing machine
乾洗	dry-clean
皺褶	wrinkle
揉皺的	crumpled

1

生 活 實 用 例 句

1 He bleached his white shirt.
他用漂白粉漂洗他的白襯衫。

2 His mother scolded him for getting his clothes dirty.
他媽媽因他弄髒了衣服而責罵他。

3. Ben washed his face and combed his hair this morning.

班今天早上洗臉刷牙。

4. Wet the windows and then give them a good clean.

把玻璃窗弄濕，然後擦乾淨。

5. There are piles of dirty laundry in the room.

房間裡有好大一堆待洗的衣物。

6. If you hang your clothes out in the bright sun, they will fade.

如果你把衣服掛在太陽底下，它們就會褪色！

7. I shrank my sweater by putting it in the dryer!

我把我的毛衣放在乾衣機裡縮水了！

2 相關單字

變乾	get dry
曬衣服	dry clothes in the sun
陰乾	dry in shade

3 慣用語句

以 pre 為首的英文單字

說明 pre-表示「事先」、「先前」的意思。

應用 事先縮水處理 preshrunk 事先浸泡

presoak	預習
preview	預測
predict	預防
precaution	

Unit 055 整理衣物

衣服	clothes
摺疊(衣物等)	fold
捲起(衣物等)	roll
展開(捲起物)	unroll
打包行李	pack
打開行李	unpack
熨、燙衣服	press
蒸汽熨斗	steam iron
熨斗	flatiron
熨衣板	ironing board

吊掛	hang
收放	put
衣櫃	closet
五斗櫃	chest of drawers
抽屜	drawer
掛衣架	hanger
衣夾	clothespin

1 生活實用例句

1 He's pressing his jacket.

他在燙外套。

2 He took his clothes out of the dryer and carefully folded them.

他把他的衣服從乾衣機裡拿出來然後折疊好！

3 She folded up the map and put it back in her bag.

她把地圖折好放進她的袋子裡！

4 She rolled up her pants so they wouldn't get wet.

她捲起褲管以免弄濕！

5 Where did you put my coat?

你把我的外套放在哪裡？

6 I keep my socks in the bottom drawer of my dresser.

我把襪子放在我的櫃子的抽屜底部！

7 There is a wooden closet in my room.

我房間裡有一個木製的衣櫃。

2 相關單字

摺疊者	folder
掛東西的人	hanger
燙熨衣服的人	ironer

3 慣用語句

以 un 為首的英文單字

說明 un-表示「不要」、「沒有」的意思。

應用 unpack　　打開行李unfold 攤開（折疊的東西等）

Unit 056 住屋

房子	house
公寓	apartment
套房	suite
分層的公寓	flat
透天房屋	townhouse
宿舍	dormitory
農舍小別墅	cottage
農場住宅	farmhouse
別墅	country house
莊園(有別墅、馬廄、泳池)	estate
避暑別墅	summer house
旅社	hostel

1 相關單字

建築物	building
摩天樓	skyscraper
寄宿家庭	home stay
青年旅舍	youth hostel
社區	community

2 慣用語句

▶ concrete jungle
水泥叢林

說明 現代都市常見的「水泥叢林」，表
示城市到處都是混凝土高樓，就是
從英文「水泥」+「叢林」直譯而
來的。

例 This city is a concrete jungle.
這是一個水泥叢林的城市。

房間	room
大廳	lobby
客廳	living room
衣帽間	walk-in closet
餐廳	dining room
餐具室	pantry
起居室	parlor
臥室	bedroom
客房	guest room

廚房	kitchen
浴廁	bathroom
車庫	garage
庭院、花園	garden
閣樓	attic
地下室	basement
酒窖、地窖	cellar
儲藏室	storeroom
工作室	workshop
畫室、工作室	atelier
工具間	tool room
棚屋、工具房	shed

生 活 實 用 例 句

1 Put your toys away in your room.
　把你的玩具收好放在房間裡。

2 Where's the bathroom?
　廁所在哪裡？

3 There is a desk in the living room.
　客廳裡有一張桌子。

4 My mother is in the kitchen.
　我母親在廚房裡。

5 They are hiding in the garage.
他們藏身在車庫裡。

6 We have a vegetable garden.
我們有一個菜園。

2 慣用語句

▶ walk-in closet
衣帽間

說明 多半是歐美國家的房間設備,多半
在入門處或樓梯下方的設計,足以
容納一個人進入的空間,可吊掛放
置臨時的衣物。

Unit 058 房屋設備

室內設施	facilities
大門	front door
側門	side door
後門	back door
玄關	entrance hall
出口通道	entryway
通道	aisle

走廊	corridor
門廊	porch
樓層	floor
樓梯	stairs
窗戶	window
台階	step
樓梯間	staircase
天花板	ceiling
陽台	balcony
欄杆	banisters
門鈴	doorbell
信箱	mailbox
屋頂	roof
車道	driveway
(從家中車庫至馬路上)	
煙囪	chimney
壁爐	fireplace

一樓	first floor
二樓	second floor
三樓	third floor
四樓	fourth floor
五樓	fifth floor
六樓	sixth floor

七樓	seventh floor
八樓	eighth floor
九樓	ninth floor
十樓	tenth floor
十一樓	eleventh floor
十二樓	twelfth floor
十三樓	thirteenth floor
十四樓	fourteenth floor
十五樓	fifteenth floor
螺旋式樓梯	spiral staircase
挑高的天花板	cathedral ceiling

  2 慣用語句

▶ **fireplace**

壁爐

說明　常見於歐美國家的設施，壁爐就是「要生火的地方」，英文就叫做 fireplace。

例　She swept the ashes from the fireplace.
她清掃壁爐內的灰燼。

Unit 059 房間內的佈置

裝置、傢俱	fitting
(一套)傢俱	suite
佈置	furnish
裝飾、佈置	decorate
裝潢	decoration
裝飾、美化	ornament
配齊、裝備	armchair
紗門	screen door
紗窗	screen
窗簾、門簾	curtain
窗簾	drape
窗架	bars
門簾、帷幕	hangings
壁紙	wallpaper
草蓆、墊子	mat
墊、椅墊	cushion
地板	floor
磁磚	tile
地毯	carpet
電燈、燈、燈光	light
檯燈	lamp

植物	plant
花盆	plant pot
油漆	paint
圖畫	picture

1 相關單字

門把	doorknob
門閂	bolt
八角窗	bay window
落地窗	French window
(窗/門上的)遮陽篷	awning
百葉窗	shutters
小地毯	rug
全鋪地毯	wall-to-wall carpet
玻璃拉門	sliding glass door
硬木地板	hardwood floor
大理石地板	marble floor
頂篷、天篷	canopy

2 慣用語句

▶ wallpaper

壁紙

說明 簡單解釋「壁紙」就是「貼在牆壁
的紙」，英文就是 wallpaper。

相關 a roll of wallpaper 一捲壁紙

例 We'd put up some wallpaper in the children's bedroom to make it brighter.
我們會在小孩房間貼上壁紙,好讓空間明亮一些。

Unit 060 傢俱

傢俱	furniture
電視櫃	TV cabinet
沙發	sofa
中小型沙發	settee
茶几	tea table
桌子	table
躺椅	couch
長沙發椅、沙發床	divan
坐臥兩用椅	recliner
涼椅	lawn chair
搖椅	rocking chair
躺椅	lounge chair
板凳	stool
旋轉凳子	swivel stool
高腳椅	high chair

長椅	bench
高背長椅	settle
導演椅	deckchair
腳墊椅	footrest
碗櫥	cupboard
櫥櫃、櫃子	cabinet
食具櫃	sideboard
書架	bookstand
書櫃	bookcase
工作臺	worktable
CD 架	CD tower
視聽架	entertainment center
儲物陳列櫥	storage cabinet
屏風	screen
(櫃子內的)層板	shelf

1 相關單字

一套傢俱	a suite of living-room furniture
一件傢俱	a piece of furniture
固定層板	fixed shelf
可調式層板	adjustable shelf

生活單字 萬用手冊

2 慣用語句

▶ recline
將椅背後仰

說明 要將座位往後仰該怎麼說？就叫做 recline the seat

例 Can I recline my seat?
我可以將椅子往後仰嗎？

Unit 061 臥室

臥房	bedroom
單人房	single room
雙人房	double room
床	bed
吊床	hammock
床頭板	headboard
床架	bedstead
床墊	mattress
枕頭	pillow
枕頭套	pillowcase
床單	sheet

床單	bedspread
鋪蓋	bedclothes
蚊帳	mosquito net
毯子	blanket
毛毯	wool blanket
棉被	comforter
被子	quilt
草蓆	mat
衣櫥	closet
床頭櫃	night table
梳妝台	dresser
五斗櫃	bureau
五斗櫃	chest of drawers
床頭燈	bedside-lamp
夜燈桌	night table
夜光燈	night light

1 相關單字

有兩張單人床的雙人房	twin-bed room
有一張雙人床的雙人房	double-bed room
雙人床	double bed
特大號的雙人床	king-size bed
大號的雙人床	queen-size bed
上下雙層床	bunk bed

單人床	single bed
2張單人床	twin bed
有腳輪的矮床	trundle bed

2 慣用語句

► single
單獨一個

說明 single 除了表示「單身」之外，也可以是「單獨一個」的意思。

應用 single parent 單親父母
single room 單人房
single bed 單人床

例 He's been single for so long.
他已經單身很久了！

Unit 062 書房

書房	study
書桌	desk
書櫃	bookcase
書架	bookstand
抽屜	drawer

檔案櫃	file cabinet
檯燈	lamp
椅子	chair
電腦	computer
筆記型電腦	notebook
電腦螢幕	monitor
鍵盤	keyboard
滑鼠	mouse
滑鼠墊	mouse pad
投影機	projector
投影片	transparency
幻燈片	slide
電話	telephone
電話答錄機	voice machine

1

生活實用例句

1. There is a pen under the desk.
   桌子底下有一枝筆。
2. My computer is broken.
   我的電腦壞了。
3. May I use your telephone?
   我可以借用你的電話嗎？

4　The art history professor showed us slides of the Parthenon today.

歷史藝術教授今天給我們看巴森農神殿的幻燈片。

5　The slide projector is not working.

投影機壞了。

2 相關單字

大辦公桌	partners desk
寫字桌	writing desk
電腦桌	computer desk
會議桌	conference table
角落電腦桌	corner computer desk

3 慣用語句

▶ stay up

熬夜

說明 stay 是「停留」、「繼續」、「忍住」的意思，stay up 則是常用片語「熬夜」。

例 She stayed up reading until midnight.

她熬夜看書到半夜才睡。

文具用品

文具	stationery
筆	pen
鉛筆	pencil
鉛筆盒	pencil case
墨水	ink
筆套	cap
筆桿	penholder
筆筒	pencil can
削鉛筆機	pencil-sharpener
橡皮擦、黑板擦	eraser
膠水	glue
修正液	correction fluid
釘書機	stapler

1 相關單字

毛筆	hair pencil
自動鉛筆	mechanical pencil
鋼筆	fountain pen
原子筆	ball-point pen
蠟筆、粉筆	crayon
墨水台	inkstand

2 慣用語句

▶ eraser

橡皮擦、黑板擦

說明 eraser 是由 erase 延伸而來的，是
「擦掉」、「抹去」的意思。

例 Did you see my eraser, Ben?

班，你有看見我的橡皮擦嗎？

Unit 064 辦公、書房用品

書籍	book
百科全書	encyclopaedia
報紙	newspaper
雜誌	magazine
紙張	paper
迴形針	clip
大頭針	pin
筆記本	notebook
活頁式的	loose-leaf
活頁簿	loose-leaf note-book
簿冊、相簿	album

日曆	calendar
卡片	card
地址本	address book
備忘錄	memo
便利貼	sticker
文件夾	file
文書夾	folder
活頁夾	binder
公文格	tray
紙夾	paper clips
膠帶	tape
尺	ruler
剪刀	scissors
圓規	compasses
美工刀	cutter knife
折信刀	letter knife
打孔機	puncher
印章	seal
印泥	inkpad
世界地圖	world map
地球儀	globe
羅盤	compass
黑板	blackboard
粉筆	chalk
橡皮筋	elastic band

1 相關單字

計算機	calculator
傳真機	fax machine
影印機	copy machine
列印機	printer
碎紙機	scrap machine
一張紙	a piece of paper
兩張紙	two sheets of paper

2 慣用語句

▶ a pair of
一雙

說明 pair 是「一雙」、「一對」或「兩個」的意思，適用在兩個一組的對象，像是鞋子、襪子、褲子、圓規、剪刀、手套等。of 後面所接的名詞為複數形態。

應用
a pair of compasses	一個圓規
a pair of scissors	一把剪刀
a pair of pants	一條褲子
a pair of gloves	一雙手套
a pair of shoes	一雙鞋子

浴室	bathroom
淋浴、淋浴間	shower
刮鬍子	shave
洗臉盆、廁所	lavatory
水龍頭	tap
水龍頭、旋塞	faucet
熱水水龍頭	hot-water faucet
冷水水龍頭	cold-water faucet
洗臉槽	basin
水槽	sink
浴缸	bath tub
澡盆、浴盆	tub
蓮蓬頭	showerhead
鏡子	mirror
毛巾架	towel-rail
毛巾桿架	towel rack
浴室窗簾	shower curtain
抽水馬桶	toilet
馬桶蓋	stool lid
馬桶座	toilet seat
把手	handle

水箱	water tank
排水管	drain
栓子	stopper
橡膠吸盤 (弄通堵塞管道用的)	plunger

1 生活實用例句

1. I left the napkins soaking in a basin.

   我在洗臉槽中浸泡餐巾。

2. Our bathroom is the warmest room in the house.

   我們的臥室是全室最溫暖的房間。

3. He carefully shaved around the cut on his cheek.

   他小心地刮臉頰上傷口旁的鬍子。

4. I gave the dog a bath.

   我有幫狗洗澡了！

5. He stays in the shower until there is no more hot water!

   他一直待在淋浴間裡直到沒有熱水為止。

6. The rear-view mirror of my car was broken.

   我車子的後照鏡壞了！

7 I need to go to the toilet.

我需要去上個廁所。

8 Did you flush the toilet?

你有沖馬桶了嗎？

2 相關單字

淋浴	take a shower
洗澡	take a bath

3 慣用語句

▶ shower

可不是只有淋浴的意思

說明 shower 除了是「淋浴」的解釋之
外，也是某些具特定意義的送禮的
意思。

應用 baby shower
慶祝將要出生的嬰兒的 party
bridal shower
為準新娘慶祝婚禮開的 party
wedding shower
慶祝婚禮而開的party

例 We're going to attend Brenda's bridal
shower.

我們要去參加布蘭迖的婚前派對。

Unit 066　浴廁裡的小用品

背刷	back brush
馬桶刷	toilet brush
肥皂	soap
肥皂台	soap stand
浴帽	shower cap
水桶	bucket
水瓢	ladle
垃圾桶	garbage can
廁所紙	toilet paper
衛生紙	tissue
衛生紙滾筒	toilet paper roll
衛生紙架	toilet paper holder

Unit 067　日常生活用品

日常用品	utensil
物品	stuff
古董	antique

鏡子	mirror
電燈	light
打火機	lighter
手電筒	flashlight
火柴	match
溫度計	thermometer
煙灰缸	ashtray
垃圾桶	trash can
時鐘	clock
雜物箱	litter box
殺蟲劑	pesticide
捕獸機	trap
裝置	device
磅秤	scale
電池	battery (複數 batteries)
乾電池	dry battery
急救箱	emergency box
工具設備	tool kit
花瓶	vase
檯燈	lamp
燈罩	lampshade

1 生活實用例句

1. We helped him move his stuff to the new apartment.

   我們幫助把他的東西搬到新公寓。

2. I've got a lot of stuff to do this weekend.

   這週我有很多事要做。

3. Buy a box of match on your way home.

   你回家的路上買一盒火柴吧！

4. There is a clock on the wall.

   牆上有一面鐘。

5. What size battery do you need for the alarm clock?

   鬧鐘需要幾號電池？

6. Excuse me, have you got a light?

   抱歉，可以借個火嗎？

7. A bear was caught in the trap.

   捕獸器抓到了一隻熊。

8. He invented a device for measuring very small distances exactly.

   他發明一種可以很精準地測量很小的距離的裝置。

2 相關單字

吊燈	pendant
落地燈	floor lamp
穹頂燈	dome light
螢光燈	fluorescent lamp
長日光燈	striplight
日光燈管	fluorescent tube
燈泡	light bulb
電燈泡	electric bulb
自動開關感應燈	sensor switch automatic light
燈光感應器	light sensor
緊急照明燈	emergency power failure light
燈絲	heater

3 慣用語句

lamp 和 light 的不同

說明 lamp 和 light 都有「燈」的含意，但是 lamp 偏向具體的燈具，而 light 則可以泛指「燈光」、「燭火」的意思。

例 Turn off the lights when you leave.
離開時把燈熄掉。

例 There is a floor lamp in the living room.

客廳裡有一盞落地燈。

Unit 068 個人清潔用品

盥洗用品	toiletry
毛巾	towel
浴巾	bath towel
洗髮精	shampoo
潤髮乳	conditioner
沐浴乳	shower gel
洗面乳	facial cleanser
牙刷	toothbrush
牙刷架	toothbrush holder
牙膏	toothpaste
牙粉	toothpowder
漱口水	mouthwash
牙線	dental floss
牙籤	toothpick
耳挖	earpick

耳塞	earplugs
刮鬍刀	razor
電動刮鬍刀	electric razor
安全剃刀	safety razor
刮鬍刀片	razor blade
刮鬍泡沫	shaving cream
乳液	lotion
身體乳液	body lotion
護手霜	hand moisturizer
腋下防臭劑	deodorant
衛生棉	sanitary napkin

1 生活實用例句

1 She came downstairs after her shower, wrapped in a towel.

淋浴後，她包著浴巾走下樓。

2 The dog needs a shampoo.

這條狗需要洗個澡了。

3 She applied some hand lotion and rubbed it in.

她塗抹一些護手霜然後揉捏。

2 相關單字

指甲剪	nail clipper
指甲銼	nail file
眉毛夾子	tweezers
梳子	brush
排骨梳	comb
細齒梳	toothcomb
髮夾	hair clip
髮型定型液	hairspray

3 慣用語句

▶ teeth
牙齒（複數）

說明 tooth 和 foot 的複數分別為 teeth 以及 feet。

例 I brush my teeth twice a day.
我每天刷牙兩次。

例 I had to have a tooth pulled.
我要去拔牙了。

電器

電視機	TV set
手提電視機	portable TV set
螢幕	screen
電視天線	TV antenna
錄放影機	VCR
電唱機	record player
留聲機	phonograph
立體電唱機	stereophonic phonograph
音響	stereo
擴音機	speaker
收音機	radio
錄音機	tape recorder
卡帶	cassette
耳機	earphone
耳機(附麥克風)	headset
頭戴式耳機	headphones
麥克風	microphone
定時開關	time switch
走動式對講機	walkie-talkie

電話答錄機	answering machine
來電顯示器	caller id
手機	cellular phone
無線電話	cordless phone
網路電話	internet phone
擴音喇叭	speakerphone
空調	air-conditioning
中央空調	central air-conditioning
中央暖氣系統	central heating
電熱器	electric heater
暖氣機	heater
風扇	fan
空氣清淨機	air cleaner
增濕機	humidifier
除濕機	dehumidifier
冷氣機	air conditioner

1 生活實用例句

1 I spend most of the day working in front of a computer screen.

我花了大部分的時間在電腦螢幕面前工作。

2 I switched on the radio.

我打開了收音機。

3 I left my cellular phone in a taxi.

我把手機遺忘在計程車裡了！

2 相關單字

電器行	electric shop
電燈開關	light switch
開關	switch
插頭、插座	plug
保險開關	cutout

3 慣用語句

▶ turn

旋轉開關按鈕

說明 打開電器電源可不是用 open 這個
單字，而是 turn on，而關閉電源則
用 turn off，舉凡電器、瓦斯聲音等
都適用。

相關 turn down　　轉小聲
　　　 turn up　　　轉大聲

例 Please turn off the lights when you
leave.

離開的時候請關燈。

例 Who turned my computer on?
誰打開我的電腦？

例 Turn up the volume -- I can't hear what
you're saying.
調高音量吧，我聽不見你在說什麼。

Unit 070 五金工具

五金工具	ironware
工具	tool
工具箱	toolbox
工作臺	bench
鐵鎚、鎯頭	hammer
釘子	nail
螺絲起子	screwdriver
螺絲釘	screw
螺絲帽	nuts
公螺絲	male screw
母螺絲	female screw
螺栓、(門等的)插銷	bolt
曲頭釘	brad
拔釘器	nail puller

扳手、扳鉗	wrench
鑽孔機	drill
鑿子	chisel
鑷子	nippers
鋸子	saw
鉋子	plane
銼刀	filc
鐮刀	sickle
耙	fork
鏟子、鐵鍬	shovel
鍬子	spade
長柄鋤、鍬	hoe
鶴嘴鋤	pickaxe
耙子	rake
銷釘	pin
十字鎬	pick
斧頭	ax
刷子	brush
砂紙	sandpaper
捲尺	tape measure
(螺栓的)墊圈	washer
梯子、腳凳	stepladder
電線、鐵絲	wire
繩索	rope

1 相關單字

錘打	hammer
擰	screw
鑿	chisel
鋸斷	saw
用鍬掘	spade
耙平	rake
刨平	plane
耙起	fork
用斧頭劈	ax
刷	brush

Unit 071　家事

家事	housework
差事	errand
丟掉	throw
清空	empty
綁住	bundle
打蠟	wax
地板上蠟	floor wax

使光亮	polish
塑膠袋	plastic bag
空氣芳香劑	air freshener
垃圾	trash
(多半為廚餘的)垃圾	garbage
髒污	dirty
污漬	blot
割草機	lawn mower

生活實用例句

1. I've no time to run errands for you.
   我沒有時間為你跑腿。

2. We filled three cans with trash from the garage.
   我們從車庫裡清出三個罐子的垃圾。

3. He left his dirty towels on the bathroom floor.
   他把髒毛巾放在浴室裡。

4. He bundled the back numbers.
   他把舊雜誌紮成一梱。

5. She threw the cheese in the garbage.
   她把起司丟進垃圾桶裡。

6 Could you show me how to use the
lawn mower?
你可以教我怎麼使用割草機嗎?

2 相關單字

把垃圾丟掉	throw the garbage away
割草	mow the yard

3 慣用語句

▶ do

可以做很多家事

說明 do 的解釋相當多,包括「製作」、
「執行」、「學習」、「烹煮」、
「洗刷」。

應用
做家事	do the housework
熨燙衣服	do the ironing
清洗	do the washing
清潔	do the cleaning
洗碗	do the dishes
寫論文	do the essay

Unit 072 家庭的清潔工作

用掃帚掃	broom
簸箕	dustpan
用拖把拖地	mop
用吸塵器吸地	vacuum
擦/刮	scrape
清洗	wash
擦拭	wipe
清潔	clear
清理	clean
除塵	dust
打掃、掃除	sweep
擰乾	wring
漂洗	rinse
耙除、掃除	rake

1 生活實用例句

1 I use that broom to sweep the kitchen floor.

我用掃把清掃廚房地板。

2 I can go as soon as I finish mopping.
只要我拖完地我就可以走了。

3 Just let me clear the dishes off the table and put them in the sink.
只要讓我清理桌上碗盤放進水槽裡。

4 You should clean a wound immediately to avoid infection.
你應該要立刻清理傷口以免感染。

5 I was dusting her desk.
我有替她的桌子除塵。

6 She sweeps the street in front of her house.
她清掃她的房子前的街道。

7 I swept under every piece of furniture.
每件家具下面我都有清掃。

8 Did you rinse out your bathing suit?
你有清洗你的泳衣嗎？

9 I have to rake up the dead leaves.
我有耙乾淨落葉。

2 相關單字

抹抹布	kitchen rag
(擦洗碗盤用的)抹布	dishcloth
(擦碟盤用的)毛巾布	dish towel
刷洗	scrub

海綿	sponge
海綿拖把	sponge mop
撢子	duster
清潔劑	detergent
肥皂	soap
漂白劑	bleach
打掃房間	sweep out the room
掃帚	broom
拖把	mop
吸塵器	vacuum

3 慣用語句

▶ mop

拖把、（用拖把）拖地

說明 有許多名詞也可以當動詞使用，像是 broom（用掃帚掃地）、vacuum（用吸塵器吸地）。

例 He mopped the bathroom floor.
他有用拖把拖過浴室的地板。

例 I vacuumed my room yesterday.
昨天我用吸塵器清掃了房間。

Unit 073 修繕工作

修繕、修補	repair
修理、校準	fix
建造、建築	build
上油漆	paint
鑽孔	drill
鋸	saw
錘打	hammer
擰	screw
鑿	chisel
鋸斷	saw
刨平	plane
耙起	fork
用斧頭劈	ax
刷	brush
丟(垃圾)	throw
捆綁	bundle

1 相關單字

給船裝桅桿	fix a mast on the boat
把架子安在牆壁上	fix a shelf to the wall
掛蚊帳	fix a mosquito net
用⋯建成	be built up of

2 慣用語句

是「看見」也是「鋸子」

說明 saw 既是 see（看見）的過去式，
也是鋸子（名詞、動詞）的意思。

相關 動詞三態　　see/saw/seen
　　　　　　　　　saw/sawed/sawed

Unit 074 城市

城市	city
城鎮	town
市中心	downtown
市中心區	urban center
縣	county
區	district
地區、場地	area
市區	urban district
郊區	outskirts
近郊之住宅區	suburb
貧民窟	slum
貧民區	shanty town
鄉村	rural area
村莊	village
住宅區	residential area
居住地點	accommodation
所在地	locality
地址	address
郵遞區號	postal code
路	road
街道	street

1
生 活 實 用 例 句

1 We live in New York City.
我們住在紐約。

2 We're going to town this Saturday.
我們打算這個星期六到城裡去。

3 There is a parking area over there.
那兒有一座停車場。

4 He has a farm on the outskirts of town.
他在市郊有一個農場。

5 They lived in a remote mountain village.
他們住在一個偏僻的山村。

6 What's your home address?
你家的地址是什麼？

7 We live on a busy road.
我們住在一條繁忙的街道。

8 Our daughter lives across the street from us.
我們的女兒就住在我們住的這條街的對面。

9 I was walking down the street when I saw David.
當我看見大衛時，我正走在街上。

2 相關單字

搬家	move
搬進	move in
搬出	move out
搬出去	move away

Unit 075 商店

商店	shop
商家	store
銀行	bank
百貨公司	department store
餐廳	restaurant
酒吧	bar
酒館、酒店	pub
咖啡館	cafe
市集	market
超級市場	supermarket
食品雜貨店	grocery
小零售店	ten-cent store
舊貨店	junk shop

書店	bookstore
報攤	newsstand
二手貨市場	secondhand market
跳蚤市場	flea market
旅館	hotel
汽車旅館	motel
藥局	pharmacy
診所	clinic

Unit 076 公共場所

公共地區	public place
首都	capital
大都市	metropolis
市中心	downtown
法院	court
銀行	bank
郵局	post office
學校	school
圖書館	library
車站	station

機場	airport
港口	port
教堂	church
大教堂	cathedral
小禮拜堂	chapel
墓地	cemetery
墳墓	grave
醫院	hospital
體育場	stadium
健身房	gym
植物園	botanical garden
紀念碑	monument
公車站	bus station
地鐵	subway
捷運站	metro station
計程車招呼站	taxi stand
停車場	parking lot
立體停車場	multilevel parking
加油站	gas station
公共廁所	comfort station

1
生活實用例句

1. Have you ever been to Yankee Stadium?

   你有去過洋基球場嗎？

2. I work out at the gym every day.

   我每天都到健身房運動。

3. While in Washington, D.C., we visited a number of historical monuments.

   在華盛頓特區時，我們參觀了很多歷史紀念碑。

4. Is there a gas station nearby?

   這附近有加油站嗎？

2
相關單字

市政廳	town hall
市政府	city hall
購物中心	shopping center
商業中心	business center
醫療中心	medical center
公共電話	public telephone

Unit 077　娛樂設施

玩耍	play
遊戲	game
遊樂場	amusement center
露天馬戲團	fairground
游泳池	swimming pool
摩天輪	Ferris wheel
旋轉木馬	merry-go-round
溜滑梯	slide
蹺蹺板	seesaw
盪鞦韆	swing
劇院	theater
電影院	cinema
俱樂部	club
圖書館	library
博物館	museum
美術館	art museum
畫廊	art gallery
動物園	zoo
公園	park
草地	lawn

學校

學校	school
大學	university
學院	college
學會、學院	institute
高中	senior high school
國中	junior high school
小學	primary school
幼童學校	infant school
幼稚園	kindergarten
托兒所	day nursery
校長辦公室	Principal's Office
圖書室	library
自然實驗室	science lab
保健室	health center
電腦教室	computer classroom
老師辦公室	teacher's office
老師	teacher
學生	student
同學	classmate
班級	class

讀書	study
畢業	graduate

1 生活實用例句

1 You should not ditch class.
你不應該蹺課。

2 We went to the same school.
我們以前是同學。

3 She graduated from the university's College of Business Management.
她從大學的商業學院畢業。

4 He graduated from high school last year.
他去年從高中畢業。

5 He is a student at the University of California.
他是加州大學的學生。

6 Ben is an English teacher.
班是英文老師。

7 David is my classmate.
大衛是我的同學。

2 相關單字

蹺課	ditch class
逃學	play hooky
沒進教室上課	skip class

3 慣用語句

▶ freshman

大學一年級

說明 「大學一年級」就叫做 freshman，也就是中文「新鮮人」的意思。

相關 sophomore　大學二年級
junior　　　大學三年級
senior　　　大學四年級

例 She is a freshman at Harvard.
她是哈佛的一年級新生。

Unit 079 交通

交通	traffic
路況報導	traffic report
交通法規	traffic laws
交通警察	traffic cops
警車	police cars
速限	speed limit
超速行車	speeding
罰款單	ticket
超速罰單	speeding ticket
違規停車罰單	parking ticket
尖峰時段交通	rush-hour traffic
抵達	arrive
等待	wait
站立	stand

1 相關單字

守法	obey the laws
違規	break the laws
匆忙中	in a rush

遵守交通規則	obey the traffic laws
違反交通規則	break the traffic laws
錯過公車	miss the bus
提早、比原定提前地	ahead of time
沒趕上火車	too late for the train

2 慣用語句

▶ ticket

是車票也是罰單

說明 ticket 不但是「車票」、「入場券」的意思，表示「罰單」之意。而「開罰單」就叫做 write a ticket。

應用 a speeding ticket　　超速罰單
　　　a parking ticket　　違規停車罰單

例 Ben got a ticket for making a U-turn on a bridge.
因為在橋上違規迴轉而吃上罰單。

Unit 080 行車狀況

駕駛車輛	drive
減速	slow down
煞車	break
迴轉	turn around
倒車	reverse
靠邊停車	pullover
左轉	turn left
右轉	turn right
通過、穿過、經過	pass
橫越	cross
橫過地	across
交通堵塞	traffic jam
車禍	car accident
小車禍	fender bender
汽車撞成一堆	pileup
(車輛的)猛撞	crash (複數為crashes)
衝撞、顛簸行進	bump
碰撞	collision
傷害、危害	injury
中斷	interruption

擁擠	congestion
繞道	detour
罰單	ticket
違規停車罰單	parking ticket
超速罰單	speeding ticket
目的地	destination

1 生活實用例句

1 He braked his car just in time to avoid an accident.

他及時煞車，避免了一次事故。

2 The collision involved a truck and a car.

貨車和汽車發生了碰撞。

3 Look both ways before you cross the street.

過馬路之前要先看一看兩邊。

4 She walked across the road.

她越過馬路。

2 相關單字

堵車	bumper-to-bumper
經過的警車	passing police cars
發生車禍	have a car accident

3 慣用語句

▶ thumb a ride
搭順風車

說明 通常在美國想要搭便車的話,用拇指指向要去的方向,即會有駕駛提供搭便車的幫助。

例 If you thumb a ride, you hitchhike.
如果你用拇指指著要去的方向,就是搭順風車的意思。

Unit 081 距離

距離	distance
哩	mile
公里	kilometer
遠/遠的	far
近/近的	close
靠近的	near
長/長的	long
短/短的	short
更遠的	farther
最遠的	farthest

更近的	closer
最近的	closest
更近的	nearer
最近的	nearest
更長的	longer
最長的	longest
更短的	shorler
最短的	shortest
走路	walk
捷徑	cut
最短路線	shortcut
(兩地之間的)直線距離	beeline

生活實用例句

1 How far is it from here?
離這裡有多遠？

2 The railway is 1000 miles long.
這條鐵路長達一千英里。

3 The post office is quite near.
郵局很近。

2 相關單字

一小時的路程	an hour's drive
一小時的步行路程	an hour's walk
五分鐘的步行路程	a five minutes' walk
走最近的路回家	take the shortest way home
一直線地	in a beeline
走一直線	take a beeline

3 慣用語句

▶ car-pool

同車共乘

說明 pool 是「游泳池」也是「集資」的意思，因此就像游泳池一樣，共乘的車子裡也可以擠滿人喔！

例 It's easier to car-pool, but you can't choose when to leave.

同車共乘很簡單，但是你不能選擇離開的時間。

速度

速度、迅速前進	speed
超速行車	speeding
加速、快的、迅速的	fast
迅速的	rapid
快的	quick
變慢、緩慢的、緩慢的	slow
快一點	faster
慢一點	slower
慢一點、減速	slow down
加速	hurry up
速限	speed limit
超速照相機	speed camera

1 生活實用例句

1 They raised the speed limit on the interstate to 65 miles per hour.

他們調高在路口的速限至時速 65 公里。

2 The ambulance sped to the hospital.
救護車急速向醫院駛去。

3 He was fined $75 for speeding.
他因為超速被罰款 75 元。

4 Don't drive so fast.
別開得這麼快。

5 That clock is ten minutes slow.
那個鐘慢了十分鐘。

6 Hurry or you'll be late.
快一點，不然你會遲到。

7 I hate to hurry you, but we have to leave in a few minutes.
我討厭一直催你，可是我們就快要離開了。

2 慣用語句

▶ fine
罰款

說明 fine 普遍的認知是「美好」、「不錯」的意思，另一個意思則有「罰款」的意思，為了要更美好，所以要用罰款來約束行為，是不是很有意思呢？也可當罰款的動詞使用。

例 He faces six months in jail and a heavy fine.
他面臨六個月牢獄及嚴重的罰金。

例 They fined him $125 for driving through a red light.

他們因為他闖紅燈而對他罰款 125 元。

Unit 083 道路

林大蔭道	avenue(縮寫 Ave.)
馬路	road(縮寫 Rd.)
街道	street(縮寫 St.)
巷	alley
弄	lane
道路(尤指車道)	roadway
迂迴路	bypass
(不收費的)高速公路	freeway
汽車專用高速公路	motorway
高速公路	expressway
超高速公路	clearway
環形交叉路口	traffic circle
支道、旁路	byway
替代道路	alternate route
四線道路	four-lane route
國道	national highway
路面、車道	pavement

小路徑	path
小徑	footpath
車行道	driveway
單行道	one-way street
單向交通	one-way traffic
人行天橋	crossover
旅客登機天橋	air bridge
人行道	sidewalk
人行天橋	skywalk
街區	block
(道路的)交叉口	intersection
走道、通道	walkway
安全島	safety island

1
生 活 實 用 例 句

1 Michigan Avenue in Chicago is famous for its elegant stores.
密西根大道在芝加哥因為雅致的商店著名。

2 David's house is down a long narrow alley.
大衛的家在一條狹長的巷子裡。

3 We drove down the muddy lane.
我們沿著泥濘的小路行駛。

4 They walked along the path
through the woods.
他們沿著林間小路走去。

5 The store is three blocks away.
那家商店距此三條街。

6 There is an accident at the
intersection of North Road and
South Road.
在北街和南街的路口有一起車禍。

2 相關單字

停車收費表	parking meter
停車格	parking space
過路費、過橋費	toll

Unit 084　交通號誌

交通信號	traffic signal
紅綠燈	traffic light
紅燈	red traffic signal
綠燈	green traffic signal
黃燈	yellow traffic signal
閃黃燈	flashing yellow traffic signal
路標	signpost
禁止大貨車進入	Not Trucks Allowed
當心行人	Watch for Pedestrians
當心殘障者	Watch for Disabled Pedestrians
禁止右轉	No Right Turn
禁止左轉	No Left Turn
禁止會車	Single Lane Only
禁止超車	No Overtaking
禁止迴轉	No U-Turn
禁止通行	No Through Road
禁止超車	No Overtaking
行人按鈕	pedestrian push-button

(紅綠燈上的裝置)	
停止行進號誌	stoplight
遠離市中心	not near the center
遠離汽車站	far from the bus stop
近火車站	near the railway station
近飛機場	near the airport

1 生活實用例句

1. The police pulled him over for failing to stop at a red traffic light.
   他因為沒有紅燈停車，被警察攔下來了。

2. Turn left at the traffic lights.
   在紅綠燈處左轉。

3. The traffic lights turned green as we approached the junction.
   我們接近路口的時候，紅綠燈就變成綠燈了。

2 相關單字

地標	landmark
市區	downtown

錐形交通路標	traffic cone
隧道	tunnel
入口	entrance
出口	exit
把⋯開到路邊	pull over

3 慣用語句

▶ pull over
停車

說明 當警察要盤查路過的車輛時，就會要求對方停車，此時警察就會說pull over.

例 A：Pull over.
把車停下來！

B：Did I do anything wrong, officer?
警官，我有做錯事嗎？

Unit 085　交通工具

自行車	bike
自行車	bicycle
輕型摩托車	motorbike
小型摩托車	scooter
機車	motorcycle
二輪馬車	cart
【美口語】三輪車	wheel
四輪馬車	carriage
車輛	vehicle
小汽車	car
汽車	automobile
轎車	sedan
小轎車	compact
雙門小轎車	coupe
敞篷車	convertible
跑車	sports car
掀背式汽車	hatchback
加長型禮車 (駕駛室與乘客席用玻璃隔開的大型轎車)	limousine
豪華轎車 (駕駛室與乘客席不隔開的汽車)	luxury sedan
客貨兩用車	wagon

生活單字 萬用手冊

休旅車	recreational vehicle(縮寫 RV)
中型的汽車	mid-size car
計程車	taxi
【美國】計程車	yellow cab
吉普車	jeep
小貨車	van
卡車	truck
拖車、【美】汽車拖的居住車	trailer

1 相關單字

貨櫃車	18-wheeler
垃圾車	garbage truck
救護車	ambulance
拖拉機	tractor
重型卡車	lorry

2 慣用語句

▶ catch my plane

趕搭我的班機

說明	catch是「趕上交通通具」的意思，像是要趕搭公車等。
應用	趕搭飛機　　catch the plane
	趕搭公車　　catch the bus

例 I don't know whether we can catch the train.

我不知道能否趕得上火車。

Unit 086 大眾運輸工具

大眾運輸工具	public transportation
公共交通運輸系統	transit
公車	bus(複數 buses)
校車	school bus
大客車	coach
地下鐵	subway
電車	trolley
鐵路	railway
捷運	metro
火車	train
纜車	tram
小船	boat
船	ship
遊艇、帆船	yacht
大船	vessel
渡輪	ferry

飛機	plane
商船	merchant ship
郵輪	ocean liner

Unit 087 車站內

車廂	class
鋪位	berth
(火車)到站停止	stop
軌道、航路	track
上船(飛機、火車等)	board
在車內	on board
站別	station
月臺	platform
月臺票	platform ticket
進入	enter
離開	leave
抵達	arrive
啟程	depart
入口	entrance
出口	exit
轉車(船、機)	transfer
轉換(車)	switch

車門	door
乘客座位區	passenger seat area
地圖	map
線路	line
路程	route
標示	signs
地鐵車門	subway car door
自動地	automatically
重新打開	reopen
(用身體)倚靠	lean
緊急鈴	Emergency Bell

Unit 088 火車、地鐵、捷運

火車	train
鐵路	railway
地下鐵	subway
捷運	metro (Mass Rapid Transit)
火車站	railway station
火車站	train station
捷運站	metro station

快車	express
電車	trolley
高架鐵路	elevated train
時刻表	timetable
頭等車廂	first class
車票(從讀卡機中)彈回	pop back
剪票箱 (地下鐵、公共汽車等的檢驗車票之處)	fare box
捷運卡讀卡機	metro card reader
十字轉門 (使人逐次通過)	turnstile
刷過 (使捷運卡被十字轉門上的機器讀取)	swipe
站務員	station agent
火車司機	engineer
(火車的)隨車服務員	conductor

生活實用例句

1 She came by train.
   她是乘火車來的。

2 Let's go by metro.
   我們搭捷運去吧！

3 The express train makes very few stops.
   快車很少停靠。

4 Why don't you take the subway to Times Square?

你何不搭地鐵去時代廣場？

Unit 089 計程車

計程車招呼站	taxi stand
計程車駕駛	taxicab driver
乘客	passenger
同行乘客	accompanying passenger
成人乘客	adult passenger
孩童乘客	chlld passenger
計程車資表	taximeter
收據	receipt
計程車費	taxi fare
通行費	toll
多點停靠	multiple stops
夜晚加收	night surcharge
車資	fare
給小費、小費	tip
零錢	change
識別證	identification

(計程車)拒載	refusal
行動不便者的服務	disability services
折收輪椅	fold up wheelchairs
放置(行李等)	place

1 相關單字

載我至某地	get me out
搭計程車	take a taxi

2 慣用語句

▶ where to
去哪裡?

說明 where to 是計程車司機用語,是問乘客目的地為何處的意思。

例 A：Where to?
　　要去哪裡?

　　B：Taipei railway station, please.
　　請送我到台北火車站。

Unit 090 公車

公車	bus
公共汽車站	bus station
公車站牌	stop
站立	stand
售票員	conductor
投放(車錢)	deposit
車票	ticket
月票	pass
公車票價	bus fare
雙層巴士	double-decker bus
上層 (雙層公共汽車的上層)	upper deck
下層 (雙層公共汽車的下層)	lower deck
遊覽車	tour bus
代幣	token
現金	cash
硬幣	coin
拉環	hand strap
公車車道	bus lane

1
生活實用例句

1. I met him on the bus yesterday.
   昨天我在公車上碰見他。

2. Have you bought your ticket yet?
   你買票了嗎？

3. The tour bus was the easiest way to Times Square.
   遊覽車是最快到時代廣場的方法。

4. He bought some tokens for the subway.
   他買了一些乘地鐵用的輔幣。

2
相關單字

搭乘公共汽車	take bus
下(車)	get off
上(車)	get on

機車、自行車

自行車	bicycle
機車	motorcyclc
自行車	bike
騎上(馬或自行車)	mount
平衡	balance
(自行車等的)把手	handlebar
座墊	seat
煞車	brake
齒輪	gear
(自行車等的)踏板	pedal
安全帽	helmet
(五指分開的)手套	gloves
膝蓋護墊	knee pad
手肘護墊	elbow pad
自行車架	bike rack

1 生活實用例句

1 Should we bike to the park, or walk?
我們要騎自行車或走路去公園？

2 Can you ride a bicycle?
你會騎自行車嗎？

3 He goes to school by bike.
他騎自行車上學。

4 Do you often ride a bicycle?
你經常騎自行車嗎？

5 She is too little to ride a bicycle.
她年紀太小了，不能騎自行車。

6 He is learning to ride a bicycle.
他正在學騎自行車。

7 Would you teach me how to ride a bicycle?
你可以教我怎麼騎自行車嗎？

8 Chris can ride a bicycle; so can I.
克里斯可以騎自行車，我也可以。

9 He can ride a bicycle, but can't ride a motorcycle.
他會騎自行車，但是不會騎機車。

2 相關單字

騎摩托車	ride a motorcycle
騎自行車	ride a bicycle
越野車	mountain bike
騎士	biker

Unit 092　電扶梯、電梯

電扶梯	escalator
(電扶梯的)樓梯	escalator steps
扶手	handrail
電梯	elevator
電梯門	elevator door
移動	move
往上	up
向下	down

1 生活實用例句

1　I'll meet you by the up escalator on the second floor.

　　我會在二樓往上的電扶梯處和你見面。

2　Many department stores have both elevators and escalators.

　　許多百貨公司既有電梯又有電扶梯。

Unit 093 加油站

加油站	gas station
油箱	gas tank
(管子等的)噴嘴	nozzle
幫浦	pump
把…轉緊	screw on
擰緊	squeeze
把…轉開取下	unscrew
汽油	gasoline
無鉛汽油	regular
柴油	diesel
油箱	tank
滿的	full
空的	empty
燃料、加油	fuel
填滿(汽油等)	fill

1 生活實用例句

1 Fill her up.
加滿油。

2 The car is out of gas!
　車子沒油了。

3 We need gas for our car.
　我們需要幫車子加點汽油。

4 Keep your eyes open for a gas station.
　注意看有沒有加油站！

5 Try to find any gas station along the way.
　找一下路邊有沒有加油站。

6 Let's look for a gas station.
　我們找一下加油站！

7 How many gallons do you want?
　你要加幾加侖？

2 相關單字

加油	get gas
裝滿	fill up

3 慣用語句

▶ fill up
加滿油

說明 汽車「加汽油」的英文怎麼說？美國人通常都說 fill her up，注意，要用女性的 her，而不能用男性的 him 喔！

例 Fill her up, please.
請加滿油，謝謝！

Unit 094 個位數字

一	one
二	two
三	three
四	four
五	five
六	six
七	seven
八	eight
九	nine

Unit 095 二位數字

十	ten
十一	eleven
十二	twelve

十三	thirteen
十四	fourteen
十五	fifteen
十六	sixteen
十七	seventeen
十八	eighteen
十九	nineteen
廿	twenty
廿一	twenty-one
卅	thirty
卅二	thirty-two
四十	forty
四十三	forty-three
五十	fifty
五十四	fifty-four
六十	sixty
七十	seventy
八十	eighty
九十	ninety

⊙註：22～29同21是「20後面加 one」
（twenty-one）的表現。31～39、
41～49、51～59、61～69、
71～79、81～89、91～99皆屬於此
相同表達方式。

Unit 096 三位數字以上

一百	a hundred
一百廿三	one hundred and twenty-three
一千	a thousand
三千四百五十六	three thousand four hundred and fifty-six
一萬	ten thousand
十萬	one hundred thousand
一百萬	a million
一千萬	ten million
十億	billion

1 生活實用例句

1 I have a two-month-old baby.
我有一個兩個月大的孩子。

2 She's now in her first year at Washington University.
她現在是華盛頓大學一年級學生。

3 She's probably in her early forties.

她可能四十出頭吧！

4 We've driven a hundred miles in the last two hours.

這兩個小時我們已經開了一百公里了。

5 "How many children are there in the school?" "About thrce hundred."

「學校裡有多少小孩子？」「大約有三百人。」

6 That dress costs hundreds of pounds.

那件裙子要價好幾百英鎊。

2 慣用語句

▶ hundreds of
數以百計

說明 口語化用法，表示數量很多的意思。hundreds 要用複數形式表示。

例 There were hundreds of people at the pool today.

今天游泳池裡有數以百計的人。

Unit 097 序號

第一	first(縮寫 1st)
第二	second(縮寫 2nd)
第三	third(縮寫 3rd)
第四	fourth(縮寫 4th)
第五	fifth(縮寫 5th)
第六	sixth(縮寫 6th)
第七	seventh(縮寫 7th)
第八	eighth(縮寫 8th)
第九	ninth(縮寫 9th)
第十	tenth(縮寫 10th)
第十一	eleventh (縮寫 11th)
第十二	twelfth(縮寫 12th)
第十三	thirteenth (縮寫 13th)
第十四	fourteenth (縮寫 14th)
第十五	fifteenth (縮寫 15th)
第十六	sixteenth (縮寫 16th)
第十七	seventeenth (縮寫 17th)

第十八	eighteenth (縮寫 18th)
第十九	nineteenth (縮寫 19th)
第二十	twentieth (縮寫 20th)
第二十一	twenty-first (縮寫 21st)
第二十二	twenty-second (縮寫 22nd)
第二十三	twenty-third (縮寫 23rd)
第三十	thirtieth(縮寫 30th)
第四十	fortieth(縮寫 40th)
第五十	fiftieth(縮寫 50th)
第六十	sixtieth(縮寫 60th)
第七十	seventieth (縮寫 70th)
第八十	eightieth (縮寫 80th)
第九十	ninetieth (縮寫 90th)
第一百	a hundredth (縮寫 100th)
第一千	a thousandth (縮寫 1,000th)
第一百萬	a millionth (縮寫 1,000,000th)

1 生活實用例句

1 This is my first visit to New York.
   這是我第一次來紐約。

2 I fell in love with him the first time I saw him.
   當我第一次看見他時，我就愛上他了。

3 I'm always nervous for the first few minutes of an exam.
   考試的前幾分鐘我總是會很緊張。

4 Who finished first?
   誰第一個完成的？

5 When did you first meet each other?
   你們第一次見面是什麼時候？

6 She was one of the first to arrive.
   她是第一個抵達的人。

7 She's now in her second year at Seattle University.
   她現在是西雅圖大二年級學生。

2 相關單字

最後的	final
最後一個	last
一次	once
兩次	twice
三次	thrice
四次	four times

Unit 098 日期

日期	date
年	year
閏年	leap year
世紀	century
十年的時間	decade
月份	month
日子	day
星期、週	week
週末	weekend
平日	weekday
日曆	calendar

曆月	calendar month
曆年	calendar year
西元前…年	B.C.
西元…年	A.D.

1

生活實用例句

1 What's today's date?
今天幾月幾號？

2 Today's date is the 24th of June.
今天是六月廿四日。

3 What is your date of birth?
你生日是什麼時候？

4 We've agreed to meet again at a later date.
我們已經同意過幾天再見面。

5 I'd like to fix a date for our next meeting.
我要安排我們下一次見面的日期。

6 Thank you for your letter dated August 30th.
感謝你八月卅日的來信。

7 Mr. Baker worked in Italy for two years.
貝克先生在義大利工作過兩年的時間。

8　We went to Egypt on holiday last year.

我們去年去埃及度假。

9　Rome was founded in the eighth century B.C.

羅馬是西元前八世紀興建的。

10　We go to the movies about once a week.

我們一星期去看一次電影。

11　The problem with the TV started a week ago Monday.

電視的問題在一週前的星期一就發生了。

12　The bank is open from 9 a.m. to 4 p.m. on weekdays.

銀行平常從早上九點營業到下午四點。

13　Do you have anything planned for the weekend?

你週末有什麼計畫嗎？

2 相關單字

需要工作的日子	work week
一週以前	a week ago
每一週	week after week
一天又一天	day by day
行動開始預定日	D-Day

3 慣用語句

▶ date
日期、約會

說明 date 除了表示「日期」之外，還可以表示「約會」、「約會的對象」（通常指男女間的約會），也可當約會的動詞使用。

例 I'll have a date tonight.
今晚我有個約會。

例 They dated for five years before they got married.
他們結婚前已經交往五年了！

Unit 099 時間

時鐘	clock
手錶	watch (複數 watches)
時間	time
鐘點	o'clock
小時	hour

分鐘	minute
秒鐘	second
準時	on time
即時	in time
早的	early
遲的、晚了的	late
延誤	delay
匆忙	rush
在…時間之前的	by
在某一段時間內	during
(火車等)趕上時間	make time
節省時間	save time
浪費時間	waste time
發車時間	train time

1 相關單字

多久的時間	how long
一個多星期	one more week
當…時候、一旦…時	as soon as
一個小時內	in an hour

2 慣用語句

▶ kill time
消磨時間

說明 殺時間?別懷疑,kill time 就是「消磨時間」以等待某事的意思。或是直接在 kill 後面加時間。

衍生 kill an hour
有一個小時的時間可以消磨

例 We had an hour to kill before going to dinner.

晚餐前我們有一個小時的時間可以消磨。

例 The train was late, so I killed an hour or so window-shopping.

火車誤點了,所以我逛街逛了一個小時。

Unit 100 星期

週、一星期、工作日	week
星期一	Monday (縮寫 Mon.)
星期二	Tuesday (縮寫 Tue.)
星期三	Wednesday (縮寫 Wed.)
星期四	Thursday (縮寫 Thu.)
星期五	Friday(縮寫 Fri.)
星期六	Saturday (縮寫 Sat.)
星期日	Sunday(縮寫 Sun.)

1 生活實用例句

1 We go to the movies about once a week.

我們大約一星期看一次電影。

2 Many offices operate on a thirty-five hour week.

許多公司一個星期工作 35 小時。

3 The first performance of the play is a week from tomorrow.

這齣戲的第一場戲從明天開始為期一週。

4 We're usually too tired to do much socializing during the week.

我們一整個星期的上班時間經常要社交實在是很累人！

5 I start my new job on Monday.

我週一開始新工作上班。

6 They go to church on Sundays.

他們星期天上教堂！

2 相關單字

上星期	last week
下星期	next week
上星期一	last Monday
下星期一	next Monday
每一週	weekly
週刊	a weekly magazine

3 慣用語句

▶ Sunday driver
駕駛技術不佳者

說明 俚語用法,泛指那些平常不開車,
只有週末才開車,卻因為不擅開車
或車速過慢而影響交通的駕駛。

例 I was eager to get there, but I got stuck
behind one Sunday driver.
我急著要去那裡,可是我被一個開車很
慢的人擋著。

Unit 101 月份

月份	month
一月	January (縮寫 Jan.)
二月	February (縮寫 Feb.)
三月	March(縮寫 Mar.)
四月	April(縮寫 Apr.)
五月	May
六月	June(縮寫 Jun.)
七月	July(縮寫 Jul.)

八月	August(縮寫 Aug.)
九月	September (縮寫 Sept.)
十月	October(縮寫 Oct.)
十一月	November (縮寫 Nov.)
十二月	December (縮寫 Dec.)

Unit 102　金錢

金錢	money
現金	cash
零錢	change
硬幣	coin
紙鈔	bill
塑膠貨幣(信用卡)	plastic
信用卡	credit card
(美金)一角硬幣	dime
元	dollar
分	cent
二十五美分	quarter
(美金)五角硬幣	fifty-cent piece
(美金)五角硬幣	half-dollar

(美金)五分錢鎳幣	nickel
(美金)一分硬幣	penny
(美金)二角五分硬幣	quarter
財力、資金	finance
資金、基金	fund
借	borrow
出借	lcnd
歸還	return
貸款	loan

生活實用例句

1 I need a dollar – have you got any money on you?

我需要一塊錢，你身上有錢嗎？

2 There's not much money in our savings account.

我們帳戶裡沒有多少錢。

3 We spent a lot of money redecorating the house.

我們花了很多錢裝潢房子。

4 The job wasn't exciting, but the money was good.

這個工作不刺激，但是薪水還不錯。

5 Can you lend me a few dollars?

你可以借我一些錢嗎？

6 Do you have change for one thousand dollars?

你有一千元的零錢嗎？

7 He loaned me twenty dollars.

他借給我二十元。

2 相關單字

存錢	save
存款	deposit
提款	withdrawal
支票	check
簽名	signature
儲蓄帳戶	savings account

3 慣用語句

▶ **use your telephone**

借打電話

說明 「借打電話」的英文可不能用 borrow 當動詞，而是著重在「借你的電話來『使用』」的思考邏輯。

例 May I use your telephone?

可以借我打個電話嗎？

Unit 103　商業貿易

投資	investment
報價單	quotation
股份、股票	share
債券	bond
利息	interest
折扣	discount
保險	insurance
抵押	mortgage
供應、補給	supply
成本、費用	cost
開支、支出	expenditure
收入、收益	income
利潤、收益	earnings
貿易、交易	commerce
商業、買賣	trade
進口	import
出口	export
專案、細目	item
購買、進貨	purchase
銷售	sale
競爭	competition

消費	consumption
需求	demand
銷路、商店	outlet
報價、出價	offer
壟斷	monopoly
預測	forecast
預算	budget
估價	estimate
日記簿	journal
交易額	turnover
虧空	deficit
總數、全額	sum
總數、總值	amount
匯票	check
收據	receipt
補貼、發給津貼	allowance
(政府的)補助金	subsidy

1 相關單字

| 治裝補貼 | clothing allowance |
| 家庭補貼 | family allowance |

稅、課稅	tax （複數taxes）
稅、關稅	duty
稅率	tax rate
執照稅	excise
扣稅前	before tax
扣稅後	after tax
所得稅	income tax
盈利稅	profit tax
財產稅	property tax
遺產繼承稅	inheritance tax
營業稅	business tax
土地稅	land tax
地方稅	local tax
納稅人	taxpayer

生活實用例句

1 Every citizen must pay taxes.
每個公民都必須納稅。

2 相關單字

收入稅額	income tax
銷售稅額	sales tax
社會安全稅額	Social Security tax
香菸稅	cigarette tax
汽油稅	gasoline tax

3 慣用語句

▶ duty-free

免稅的、免稅商品

說明 free 是免費的意思，duty-free 字面意思是「不用稅」可當名詞及形容詞使用。

例 I almost missed my flight because there was a long queue in the duty-free shop.

我差一點錯過班機，因為免稅商店排隊結帳的人太多了！

例 We can buy our duty-free while we're waiting at the airport.

我們在機場候機的時候，可以買一些免稅商品。

國家

國內的	domestic
國外的	overseas
海外	abroad
中華民國	the Republic of China
中國大陸	Mainland China
日本	Japan
韓國	Korea
北韓	North Korea
菲律賓	Philippines
泰國	Thailand
緬甸	Myanmar
印尼	Indonesia
印度	India
越南	Vietnam
美國	America
加拿大	Canada
英國	Britain
英國	England
愛爾蘭	Ireland
法國	France

德國	Germany
比利時	Belgium
瑞士	Switzerland
義大利	Italy
西班牙	Spain
希臘	Greece
匈牙利	Hungary
波蘭	Poland
荷蘭	Netherlands
俄國	Russia
澳大利亞	Australia
紐西蘭	New Zealand
南非	South Africa
埃及	Egypt
哥倫比亞	Colombia
宏都拉斯	Honduras
墨西哥	Mexico
阿根廷	Argentina
巴西	Brazil
巴拿馬	Panama
土耳其	Turkey
南斯拉夫	Yugoslavia
剛果	Congo
奧地利	Austria
伊拉克	Iraq

黎巴嫩	Lebanon
阿富汗	Afghanistan
羅馬尼亞	Romania
衣索比亞	Ethiopia

Unit 106 節日

假期	vacation
假日、節日	holiday
長假	long vacation
新年	New Year
除夕	New Year's Eve
聖誕節	Christmas
聖誕除夕	Christmas Eve
復活節	Easter
萬聖節	Halloween
感恩節	Thanksgiving Day
母親節	Mother's Day
情人節	Valentine's Day

1 生活實用例句

1 People usually visit their families at Christmas.

人們通常會在耶誕節的時候拜訪家人。

2 Happy New Year!

新年快樂！

3 Merry Christmas!

耶誕節快樂！

4 The family had just left for a vacation.

這家人剛出發去度假。

5 Friday is a holiday in Muslim countries.

在回教國家裡星期五是假日。

6 He got lots of valentine cards on Valentine's Day.

他在情人節收到很多情人節卡片。

2 相關單字

假期後遺症	vacation hangover
暑假	summer vacation
寒假	winter vacation
度假村	holiday camp
復活節兔子	Easter egg

給糖就不搗蛋	trick or treat
情人節卡片	valentine card

 慣用語句

▶ on vacation

度假

說明 on vacation 的動詞可以用 be on vacation 或 go on vacation 表示。

例 We always go on vacation in August.
我們總是會在八月的時候去度假。

Unit 107 臉部

臉部	face
額頭、腦門	forehead
太陽穴	temple
顎	jaw
上顎	the upper jaw
下顎	the lower jaw
下巴	chin
牙齒	tooth (複數 teeth)
假牙	denture

牙齦	gum
舌頭	tongue
味蕾	taste bud
鬍子	mustache

1 生活實用例句

1 I brush my teeth twice a day.
　　我每天刷兩次牙。

2 He's an old man with a trim mustache.
　　他是留著小鬍子的老男人。

2 相關單字

一副假牙	a set of dentures
絡腮鬍	whisker
鬢角	sideburns
山羊鬍	beard

3 慣用語句

▶ poker face

面無表情

說明 就像撲克牌上的人物一樣面無表情，就叫 poker face。poker 是「撲克牌」的意思。

例 He kept a poker face all day long.
他一整天都面無表情。

Unit 108　五官

眉毛	eyebrow
眼睛	eye
眼窩	eyehole
眼瞼、眼皮	eyelid
睫毛	eyelashes
虹膜	iris
瞳孔	pupil
角膜	cornea
耳朵	ear
耳垂	earlobe
鼻子	nose

鼻孔	nostril
臉頰	cheek
嘴	mouth
嘴唇	lip

1 相關單字

禿頭	bald head
皺紋	wrinkle
痣	mole
雀斑	freckle
酒窩	dimple
粉刺	pimple
濕疣	condyloma

2 慣用語句

▶ pupil

小學生

說明 pupil 除了是「瞳孔」的意思外，也同樣是「小學生」的意思。

例 The school has 1500 pupils.
這所學校有一千五百名小學生。

手臂	arm
腋下	armpit
肘部	elbow
手	hand
手掌	palm
拳頭	fist
手指	finger
大拇指	thumb
食指	forefinger
中指	middle finger
無名指	ring finger
小指	little finger
手指	fingernail
指甲	nail
手腕	wrist

1 相關單字

1 He held a tiny seed between his thumb and forefinger.
他手裡捏著著一顆很小的種子。

2 She put her arm around his waist.
她把手臂環繞在他的腰。

3 He held her in his arms.
他環抱著她。

2 慣用語句

▶ lift a finger

舉手之勞

說明 表示只是「動一下手指」般的簡單。

例 He just watches TV all evening and never lifts a finger to help with the dishes.

他每天晚上都在看電視，就是不願意動一下幫忙洗碗。

Unit 110　腳部

腿	leg
大腿	thigh
腰至膝蓋	lap
膝蓋	knee
小腿	shank
小腿肚	calf
踝	ankle
腳	foot(複數 feet)
腳趾頭	toe
腳趾甲	toenail
腳背	instep
腳後跟	heel
腳底	sole

1 生活實用例句

1 He broke his leg last night.
他昨晚摔斷腿。

2 Her skirt came to just above the knee.

她的裙子長度只到膝蓋上。

3 I've got a splinter in my heel.

我的腳跟刺傷了！

4 Come and sit on my lap and I'll read you a story.

過來坐在我的腿上，我說故事給你聽。

5 She was on her knees weeding the garden.

她跪著給花園除雜草。

2 慣用語句

▶ kneel down

跪下

說明 要特別注意，kneel 的過去式是 "knelt"。

例 She knelt down to look under the bed for her doll.

她跪下來在床下找她的洋娃娃。

身體

身體	body
頭	head
腦	brain
頭髮	hair
咽喉	throat
扁桃腺	tonsil
脖子	neck
後頸	nape
皮膚	skin
胸部、乳房	chest
乳頭	nipple
【口語】乳頭	tit
腹部	abdomen
肚臍	navel
肩	shoulder
背	back
腰	waist
臀部	hip
屁股的半邊肉	buttocks
【俗語】屁股	butt

1 生活實用例句

1 She's got a long, thin face.
她有一張瘦長的臉。

2 My feet are killing me.
我的腳痛死了。

3 A cop grabbed him around the throat.
警察抓住他的喉嚨。

4 I have a sore throat.
我喉嚨痛！

5 She didn't want to talk and turned her back to him.
她不想說話並背對他。

6 The back of a seat is the part your back leans against.
椅背是你的背靠著的地方。

2 相關單字

食道	esophagus
氣管	windpipe
脊椎神經	spinal cord

3 慣用語句

▶ kick your ass
討打

說明 字面意思很簡單:「踢你的屁股」,這是一句粗俗的用法。

Unit 112 骨骼、肌肉、血管

骨	bone
骨骼	skeleton
頭蓋骨	skull
鎖骨	collarbone
肋骨	rib
脊骨、脊柱	backbone
胸骨	breastbone
關節	joint
指關節	knuckle
膝蓋骨	kneecap
骨盆	pelvis
腱	sinew
肌肉	muscle

血管	blood vessel
血管	veins
靜脈	vein
動脈	artery
毛細管	capillary
神經	nerve
脊髓	spinal marrow

Unit 113 器官、內臟

器官	organ
內臟	entrails
心臟	heart
腎臟	kidney
肺	lung
肝	liver
膽囊	gallbladder
隔膜	diaphragm
食道	gullet
胃	stomach
胰腺	pancreas
脾	spleen

十二指腸	duodenum
大腸	large intestine
小腸	small intestine
直腸	rectum
盲腸	appendix
膀胱	bladder
肛門	anus
尿道	urine
陰莖	penis
睪丸	testicle
陰囊	scrotitis
卵巢	ovary
子宮	womb
陰道	vagina

Unit 114　身體不舒服、疾病

疾病	disease
病症	symptoms
生病的	sick
頭痛	headache
暈眩的	dizzy
頭暈的、模糊的	swimmy

鼻塞、胸悶	congested
牙痛	toothache
蛀牙	cavity
打噴嚏	sneeze
臉色蒼白	pale
感冒、傷風	cold
營養不良	malnutrition
發氣喘聲、喘息	wheeze
脖子僵硬	stiff neck
胃痛	stomachache
打嗝	burp
吐	vomit
咳嗽	cough
腹瀉	diarrhea

1 相關單字

流感	flu
瘧疾	malaria
麻疹	measles
癌症	cancer
吐	throw up
覺得很好	feel well
覺得生病	feel sick
生病的	ill
疾病	illness

瞎的	blind
耳聾的	deaf

▶ go to see a doctor

看醫生

說明 字面意思很簡單，就是「去看醫生」，也就是找醫生診療的意思。

例 A: I feel headache.

我頭痛！

B：You need to go see a doctor.

你需要去看醫生。

Unit 115　受傷

使受傷	hurt
傷殘	injuries
流血	bleed
腫脹的	swollen
扭傷、挫傷	twist
使扭傷	sprain
使脫臼	dislocate

使受瘀傷/瘀青	bruise
切、剪、砍/傷口	cut
傷口、創傷	wound
折斷	break
抓、搔	scratch
擦、刮	scrape
癢/發癢	itch
發癢的	itchy

1 生活實用例句

1 She fell and broke her arm.
她跌倒摔斷了手臂。

2 I've got an itch on the back of my neck.
我脖子後面很癢！

3 The sweater was itchy.
我穿這件毛衣會很癢。

2 相關單字

疤痕	scar
痛苦	pain
叫救護車	call an ambulance

3 慣用語句

▶ get hurt

受傷

說明 hurt 是「受傷」的意思，可以當動詞、名詞或形容詞使用。

例 How did you get hurt?
你怎麼受傷的？

例 My right leg hurts.
我右腳疼。

Unit 116 症狀

流鼻血	have a bloody nose
鼻塞	have a stuffy nose
流鼻水	have a runny nose
喉嚨發炎	have laryngitis
口腔潰瘍(嘴破)	have a canker sore
牙痛	have a toothache
蛀牙	have a cavity
感染到	have an infection
起疹子	have a rash

腹瀉	have diarrhea
被蟲子咬的	got bit by an insect
曬傷	have a sunburn
打嗝	have the hiccups
寒顫	have the chills
長雞眼	have a wart
胸膛痛	have chest pain
頭痛	have a headache
眼睛痛	eyes hurt

Unit 117　治療

處方	prescription
藥、藥劑、藥物 (尤指內服藥)	medicine
成藥	over-the-counter drugs
(傷口的)包紮	dressing
注射	shot
打針、注射、灌腸	injection
抗生素	antibiotic
阿斯匹靈	aspirin
含藥糖漿(藥水)	syrup

利尿劑	diuretic
眼藥水	eye drops
通便劑、輕瀉劑	laxative
軟膏	ointment
止痛劑	painkiller
盤尼西林	penicillin
鎮定劑	sedative
安眠藥	sleeping pills
嗅鹽(治頭痛、昏厥)	smelling salts
喉片	throat lozenge
繃帶	bandages
三角巾	triangular bandage
醫治	cure
治療	treatment
復原	recover

1 相關單字

內科	medicine
外科	surgery

2 慣用語句

▶ apply a bandage

縛繃帶於

說明 bandage（繃帶）同樣是可以當成名詞和動詞使用。

相關 have a shot in the arm
在手臂上注射一針

例 He applied a bandage around his arm.
他在手臂上包紮繃帶。

例 They bandaged his wounds.
他們包紮了他的傷口。

Unit 118　美髮

頭髮	hair
洗髮精	shampoo
護髮霜	hair conditioner
髮膠	gel
定型液	hair spray
染髮劑	hair color
髮雕	lotion
燙髮	permanent
剪髮	hair cutting
染髮	hair coloring
頭髮吹乾	blowdrying
護髮	hair treatment

1 相關單字

修指甲	manicure
修腳甲	pedicure
按摩	massage
指甲保養	nail care

2 慣用語句

▶ have a haircut

剪髮

說明 剪髮不需要使用到「剪」這個英文
字，只要用 have a haircut 就可
以。

例 A：You look different.

你看起來不太一樣。

B：I had a haircut yesterday.

我昨天去剪頭髮了！

Unit 119 休閒

嗜好	hobby
興趣	interest
休閒	leisure time
享樂	enjoy
花時間	spend time
聽音樂	listen to music
旅遊	travel
爬山	mountain climbing
閱讀	reading books
交朋友	making friends
看電影	seeing movies

1 生活實用例句

1. David's hobbies include traveling, sailing, and reading novels.
   大衛的興趣包含旅遊、划船和讀小說。

2. Did you enjoy yourself?
   玩得開心嗎？

3. I went to see a movie last night.
   我昨晚去看電影。

2 相關單字

純粹好玩	for fun
象棋	chess
圍棋	go
橋牌	bridge

3 慣用語句

▶ be interested in

對…有興趣

說明 be interested in 是常用片語，in 後面要接名詞或動名詞。

例 I'm not interested in politics.
我對政治不感興趣。

Unit 120　運動

運動	sport
戶外運動	outdoor sports
室內運動	indoor sports
短跑	dash

賽跑	race
競走	walk
馬拉松	marathon
足球(美式橄欖球)	football
英式足球	soccer
籃球	basketball
排球	volleyball
羽毛球	badminton
網球	tennis
乒乓球	table tennis
棒球	baseball
拳擊	boxing
撐竿跳	pole vault
跳高	high jump
跳遠	long jump
投擲	throwing
推鉛球	shot put
鐵餅	discus
鏈球	hammer
標槍	javelin
體操	gymnastics
單槓	horizontal bar
雙槓	parallel bars
吊環	rings
舉重	weight-lifting

柔道	judo
摔角	wrestling
空手道	karate
瑜珈	yoga
擊劍	fencing
手球	handball
曲棍球	hockey
高爾夫球	golf
板球	cricket
滑雪	ski
滑雪	skiing

Unit 121 游泳

游泳	swim
蛙泳	breaststroke
仰泳	backstroke
自由式	freestyle
蝶式	butterfly stroke
狗爬泳	crawl stroke
跳台	diving platform
跳水池	diving pool
游泳池	swimming pool

泳道	swimming lane
泳衣	swimming suit
泳褲	swimming trunks
泳帽	swimming cap
比基尼泳衣	bikini
比基尼式泳褲	bikini bottom
更衣室	changing room
救生員(海上或游泳池)	lifeguard
(比賽中的)計時員	timekeeper

生活實用例句

1 He jumped in the river and swam.
他跳進河裡游泳。

2 Can you do backstroke?
你會仰式游泳嗎？

3 We go swimming every weekend.
我們每週游泳！

2 相關單字

深水池	swimmer's pool
淺水池	non-swimmer's pool
室內游泳池	an indoor swimming pool

Unit 122 水上運動

潛水、跳水	dive
潛水、跳水	diving
浮潛	snorkeling
潛水	scuba diving
水球	water polo
划船	row
划船	rowing
划艇	canoe
溜冰	skate
滑冰	skating
衝浪	surf
衝浪	surfing
滑水	water skiing
花式溜冰	figure skating
雪橇	bobsleigh
冰上曲棍球	ice hockey

1 生活實用例句

1. He dived into the river to save a drowning child.

   他跳入河中救一個溺水的小孩。

2. Ben dove off the cliff into the ocean.

   班跳下懸崖衝進海裡！

3. The submarine dived.

   潛水艇下潛了。

4. We skatd a lot when we were younger.

   我們年紀比較輕的時候經常溜冰。

5. They go surfing every weekend.

   他們每週都去衝浪！

6. If the waves are big enough, we'll go surfing.

   如果浪夠大的話，我們就會去衝浪。

2 相關單字

沖浪板	surfboard
四輪溜冰鞋	skate
溜冰鞋	ice skate

天氣預報	weather forecast
氣象學	meteorology
大氣	atmosphere
氣候	climate
天氣	weather
雲	cloud
霧、起霧	mist
霾	haze
雪、下雪	snow
霜、結霜	frost
濃霧、結霧	fog
露水、結露	dew
晨露	morning dew
冰雹、下雹	hail
雨、下雨	rain
陣雨、下陣雨	shower
潮濕	wet
雷、打雷	thunder
閃電	lightning
日光、陽光	sunlight
陽光	sunshine

風	wind
微風	breeze
季風	monsoon
潮濕	humidity
冰凍	freeze
乾旱	drought
彩虹	rainbow
洪水	flood
潮汐	tide
大雨、豪雨、暴雨	downpour
暴風雨、颳大風	storm
颶風	hurricane
旋風	cyclone
颱風	typhoon
龍捲風	tornado
地震	earthquake
山崩	landslide
海嘯	tsunami
洪水	flood
泛濫	flow

1 生活實用例句

1 My parents like the warm, dry climate of Arizona.

我的父母喜歡亞歷桑納洲溫暖、乾燥的氣候。

2 I always wear gloves in cold weather.

天氣冷時我總是會戴手套。

2 相關單字

濃霧	heavy mist
一場大雪	heavy snow
嚴霜	hard frost
一聲響雷	a clap of thunder

Unit 124 天氣狀況

晴天的	fine
晴朗的	clear
晴朗的	sunny
下雨的	rainy

陰天的	dull
潮濕的	wet
陰涼處	shade
有風的	windy
冷颼颼的	chilly
多雲的	cloudy
多霧的	foggy
露濕的	dewy
熱的	hot
溫暖的	warm
冷的	cold
涼爽的	cool
多雪的	snowy

生 活 實 用 例 句

1 We had three rainy days on holiday, but otherwise it was sunny.

除了三天的假期是雨天之外，其他時間都是晴朗的天氣。

2 It was a windy night.

晚上風很大。

3 It's getting windy.

起風了。

4 It was wet and windy for most of the week.

這星期大部分時間都是潮濕、有風的。

5 I saw him sitting in the shade of a tree.

我看見他坐在樹蔭下。

6 The sun was hot, and there were no trees to offer us shade.

太陽好大，我們實在沒有地方可以遮陰。

Unit 125　季節

季節	season
春天	spring
夏天	summer
秋天	autumn=fall
冬天	winter
氣溫	temperature
攝氏	Celsius
華氏	Fahrenheit

生活單字 萬用手冊

1
生 活 實 用 例 句

1 Shall I give you the temperature in Celsius or in Fahrenheit?
我要給你攝氏或是華氏的溫度？

2 It was 80 °F in the shade.
陰涼處是華氏八十度。

3 Are the temperatures given in Celsius or Fahrenheit?
這是攝氏還是華氏的溫度？

2 相 關 單 字

暑假	summer vacation
寒假	winter vacation
寒冬	hard winter

Unit 126　陸地、森林

大陸、陸地	continent
大陸 (與附近島嶼和半島相對而言)	mainland
島嶼、群島	island
離島	off-shore island
無人島	desert island
半島	peninsula
冰山	iceberg
冰川	glacier
大草原	prairie
高原、高地	plateau
平原	plain
高原	plateau
森林	forest
灌木叢	bush
樹木、喬木	tree
矮樹、灌木	shrub
草本植物	herb
(樹木、草等的)叢	tuft

Unit 127　山景

土壤	soil
地面	ground
小山、山崗	hill
岩石	rock
山	mountain
山峰	summit
山頂	peak
山脊	ridge
山坡	slope
懸崖峭壁	cliff
峽谷	canyon
山谷	valley
火山	volcano
火山灰	volcanic ash
熔岩	lava
沙漠	desert
流沙	quicksand

生活單字萬用手冊

親愛的顧客您好，感謝您購買這本書。即日起，填寫讀者回函卡寄回至本公司，我們每月將抽出一百名回函讀者，寄出精美禮物並享有生日當月購書優惠！想知道更多更即時的消息，歡迎加入"永續圖書粉絲團"您也可以選擇傳真、掃描或用本公司準備的免郵回函寄回，謝謝。

傳真電話：（02）8647-3660　　　　電子信箱：yungjiuh@ms45.hinet.net

姓名：		性別：　□男　□女
出生日期：　年　　月　　日	電話：	
學歷：	職業：	
E-mail：		
地址：□□□		
從何處購買此書：	購買金額：　　　　元	

購買本書動機：□封面 □書名 □排版 □內容 □作者 □偶然衝動

你對本書的意見：
內容：□滿意□尚可□待改進　　編輯：□滿意□尚可□待改進
封面：□滿意□尚可□待改進　　定價：□滿意□尚可□待改進

其他建議：

總經銷：永續圖書有限公司

永續圖書線上購物網
www.foreverbooks.com.tw

您可以使用以下方式將回函寄回。

您的回覆，是我們進步的最大動力，謝謝。

① 使用本公司準備的免郵回函寄回。

② 傳真電話：（02）8647-3660

③ 掃描圖檔寄到電子信箱：

　　yungjiuh@ms45.hinet.net

沿此線對折後寄回，謝謝。

廣 告 回 信

基隆郵局登記證

基隆廣字第056號

2 2 1 0 3

 雅典文化事業有限公司　收
新北市汐止區大同路三段194號9樓之1

雅致風靡　典藏文化